Man's capacities have never been measured; nor are we to judge of what he can do by any precedents, so little has been tried.
—Thoreau

So maybe I can't win this lousy war. But I'm going to give it one hell of a try.
—Mack Bolan, THE EXECUTIONER

# THE EXECUTIONER:
## Panic in Philly

*by*
*Don Pendleton*

PINNACLE BOOKS • NEW YORK CITY

THE EXECUTIONER: PANIC IN PHILLY

An original Pinnacle Books edition, published for the
first time anywhere.

First printing, March 1973

Printed in the United States of America

PINNACLE BOOKS, INC.
116 East 27 Street, New York, N.Y. 10016

For Jim Schmidt of Michigan,
Frank Marrone of California,
Alberta Simmons of New Jersey,
Eugene and Rosemarie Harney of Indiana—
and for the countless others who know
that their names belong here—
MB sends his thanks.

dp

OFFICIAL POLICE BUSINESS
**RESTRICTED COMMUNIQUE**
SCRAMBLE CIRCUIT AUTHY #SD105
FROM SAN DIEGO PD 120915L
TO H BROGNOLA/USDOJ/WASHDC
**IMMEDIATE ATTN**
BT
M BOLAN CONTACT REPORT AND
MOVEMENT ADVISORY.
SUBJECT BELIEVED TO HAVE
COMMENCED OPERATIONS THIS CITY
EARLY 9TH. ENGAGED LOCAL ARM
OF OLD DIGEORGE FAMILY WITH
STANDARD RESULT, SAME DEAD OR
DISBANDED AND IN FLIGHT. FULL
DETAILS FOLLOW VIA OFFICIAL MAIL.
SUBJECT APPARENTLY DEPARTED
SO/CAL AREA THIS DATE, BELIEVED
HEADED EASTERN US.
BT
TATUM SDPD SENDS
EOM

UNIFORM CRIME NETWORK—
US/DOJ—ADVISORY SPECIAL
CON/US ALERT***ALL LEA EASTERN
SEABOARD STATES***ALERT
121252L

BT

SUBJECT MACK BOLAN AKA THE EXECUTIONER LAST SURFACED AT SAN DIEGO NOW BELIEVED HEADED US EASTERN SEABD.

MODUS OPERANDI NOTED AT SAN DIEGO APPEARS SIGNIFICANTLY ALTERED FROM PREVIOUS CAMPAIGNS BUT PERHAPS ATTRIBUTABLE TO PERSONAL REASONS FOR SDIEGO VISIT. EASTERN LEA URGED INCREASED VIGILANCE, ESPECIALLY DC NY PHILA AREAS WHERE CONSIDERABLE UNDERWORLD UNREST COULD ACT AS MAGNET FOR RENEWED EXECUTIONER WAR OF SURPASSING FEROCITY.

**SPECIAL NOTE**

SINCE WASHINGTON HIT INFORMANTS REPORT HEIGHTENED AGITATION UPPER ECHELONS ORGCRIMEWORLD WITH FIRM RESOLVE TO END BOLAN MENACE ONCE AND FOR ALL. SHOULD SUBJECT SURFACE ANYWHERE IN NORTHEAST US IT IS FELT THAT SPECIALLY ACTIVATED ENFORCER GROUPS WILL BE AWAITING HIM. LEA THESE AREAS URGED EXTRAORDINARY VIGILANCE FOR QUICK REACTION FIRST SIGN OF EXECUTIONER PRESENCE AS NEW WAR COULD EXCEED ANYTHING PREVIOUSLY EXPERIENCED THIS SUBJECT.

**SPECIAL ADVICE**
PAST EXPERIENCE THIS SUBJECT
INDICATES MOST EFFECTIVE LEA
RESPONSE TO BOLAN OPERATIONS
LIES IN ISOLATION OF LOCAL
ORGCRIMEWORLD FIGURES. SUGGEST
ROUNDUP AND ARREST FIRST SIGN
OF BOLAN ACTIVITIES IN AREA.
**SPECIAL REQUEST**
PLEASE NOTIFY SENDER IMMEDIATELY
ANY CONTACT OR SUSPECTED
ACTIVITY THIS SUBJECT. USE
RESTRICTED COMMUNIQUE, SCRAMBLE
CIRCUIT AUTHORITY NO 105.
BT
BROGNOLA USDOJ SENDS
SPECIAL REPEAT BACKGROUND
ADVISORY FOLLOWS
EOM
REPEATING FOR INFO UNIFORM
CRIME NETWORK—US/DOJ—ADVISORY
SPECIAL

SUBJECT
MACK BOLAN, ALSO KNOWN AS "THE
EXECUTIONER". OPERATES ALSO
UNDER VARIOUS COVER NAMES,
USUALLY OF ITALIAN OR SICILIAN
ORIGIN. AMERICAN CAUCASIAN, AGE
30/35 HEIGHT 75 INCHES WEIGHT ABOUT
200. COLOR OF HAIR VARIES,
NORMALLY DARK. EYES BLUE, USUALLY
DESCRIBED AS ICY, PENETRATING,

OBVIOUSLY HIGHLY DEVELOPED NIGHT VISION. SOMETIMES AFFECTS COSTUME OF BLACK COMBAT GARB, COMMANDO STYLE, BUT ALSO KNOWN TO WEAR VARIOUS INNOCUOUS OUTFITS IN SUBTLE APPLICATIONS OF "ROLE CAMOUFLAGE".

CHARACTERISTICS
HAS AVOWED UNENDING WARFARE AGAINST ALL ELEMENTS OF ORGCRIMEWORLD AND FELLOW TRAVELERS EVERYWHERE. BY CONSERVATIVE ESTIMATES, HAS SLAIN MORE THAN 1,000 UNDERWORLD FIGURES. COMBAT VETERAN OF VIETNAM, HIGHLY SKILLED SPECIALIST IN "DESTRUCT MISSIONS" AGAINST ENEMY STRONGHOLDS. RECEIVED NICKNAME "THE EXECUTIONER" IN VIETNAM, THIS REGARD. CONSIDERED BY MILITARY COMMANDERS AS HIGHLY ADEPT AT PENETRATION/ INTELLIGENCE TECHNIQUES. MILITARY TACTICIAN AND STRATEGIST OF HIGHEST ORDER, GUERRILA WARFARE EXPERT, WEAPONS EXPERT, PHENOMENAL MARKSMAN. HAS BEEN KNOWN TO ALSO USE HEAVY COMBAT WEAPONS SUCH AS MORTAR, BAZOOKA, DEMOLITION DEVICES. CUSTOMARILY WEARS 9MM BERETTA BRIGADIER EQUIPPED WITH SILENCER

ALSO 44 CALIBRE AUTOLOADING MAGNUM, IMPRESSIVE FIREPOWER BOTH WEAPONS.

**CAUTION** SUBJECT IS EXTREMELY QUICK IN MILITARY STYLE STRIKE TECHNIQUES WITH EXPLOSIVE-REACTION COMBAT INSTINCTS. NON-UNIFORMED OFFICERS ADVISED NOT REPEAT NOT ATTEMPT GUNPOINT ARREST BUT SHOOT ON SIGHT, TO KILL.

**SPECIAL INFO**

SUBJECT IS IN CONTINUAL "STATE OF WAR" AND SHOULD BE CONSIDERED HIGHLY DANGEROUS. ALL LEA URGED EXERCISE EXTREME CAUTION. DO NOT ATTEMPT MAN-TO-MAN ARREST. SUBJECT APPEARS TO AVOID POLICE CONFRONTATION AND IS NOT KNOWN TO HAVE FIRED UPON LEA. SUBJECT IS DESPERATELY DEFENSIVE, HOWEVER IN CONSTANT JEOPARDY VIA VARIOUS DETERMINED UNDERWORLD ELEMENTS. RUMORED "OPEN CONTRACT" IN AMOUNTS EXCEEDING 100-THOUSDOLS ATTRACTS CONSTANT ATTENTION EVER-INCREASING FREELANCE GUNMEN. SUBJECT IS THEREFORE UNDER CONTINUAL DURESS AND IS EXTREMELY DANGEROUS TO APPROACH. VARIOUS REGIONAL LEA HAVE UNOFFICIALLY AUTHORIZED "EXTREME PRECAUTION APPREHENSION —SHOOT ON SIGHT, TO KILL!"

11

**\*\*BACKGROUND INFO\*\***
HOMETOWN FRIENDS, TEACHERS, GI
COMPANIONS, ETC DESCRIBE SUBJECT
AS MILD-MANNERED, COURTEOUS,
LIKABLE, WELL-ADJUSTED. WELSH-
POLISH EXTRACTION, ELDEST OF THREE
CHILDREN. MOTHER FATHER SISTER
VICTIMS OF VIOLENT DEATH WHILE
SUBJECT SERVING VIETNAM THEATRE.
SUBJECT GRANTED EMERGENCY
FURLOUGH BURY FAMILY AND ARRANGE
CARE OF ORPHANED YOUNGER
BROTHER. "HOMEFRONT WAR" BEGAN
DURING THIS PERIOD, OBVIOUSLY IN
REACTION TO FAMILY TRAGEDY.
FOLLOWING VICTORY OVER
HOMETOWN ORGCRIME ELEMENTS
SUBJECT PURSUED SUCCESSIVE
CAMPAIGNS IN LOSANGS, PALM SPGS,
PHOENIX, MIAMI, FRANCE, ENGLAND,
NYC, CHI, LASVEG, PUERTO RICO,
SANFRAN, BOSTON, DC. UNOFFICIAL
POLICE SYMPATHY SUSPECTED VARIOUS
QUARTERS LEA, RECOMMEND
INDOCTRINATION PROGRAMS
EMPHASIZING PUBLIC MENACE ASPECTS
OF SUBJECTS ILLEGAL CRUSADE.
RUMORS ABSOLUTELY UNFOUNDED
REPEAT UNFOUNDED AND UNTRUE
THAT VARIOUS FEDERAL AGENCIES ARE
SUPPORTING SUBJECTS PRIVATE WAR.

**\*\*FORWARD LOOK\*\***

EXCEPT FOR UNUSUAL FEINT AT ENEMY
IN SAN DIEGO, BOLAN HAS EXHIBITED
EXTREMELY LOW PROFILE SINCE
WASHDC CAMPAIGN, BELIEVED
PLANNING MASSIVE STRIKE NEAST
US REGION. UNUSUAL MOVEMENTS
ALSO NOTED ORGCRIMEWORLD
THIS REGION SUGGESTING MASSIVE
COUNTERBLOW RECEPTION FOR
EXPECTED BOLAN HIT. ALL LEA
CAUTIONS AND VIG STRONGLY URGED.
BT
BROGNOLA-US/DOJ SENDS
EOM

## Chapter 1 / *The Announcement*

Panic came to Philadelphia on a cool Spring morning and its name was Death—purposeful, clad in black as a symbol of utter finality, moving swiftly in its inevitability.

It stepped silently into the rear office of Cappy's Liberty Garage and gave the five men in there a stricken moment to see what had come for them.

Al the Mouth DiLucci was the first to unglue himself from that frozen confrontation. He yelled, "Jesus, it's—" and spun away from the stacks of money which were being counted at the battered wooden desk.

The furious chatter of a light automatic pistol cut short the final declaration of Al the Mouth, the hot little missiles from its blazing muzzle forming a shattered-flesh wreath upon his neck and shoulders as he spun into eternity.

The other four targets were lunging about in scattered patterns of flight, two of them making electrified stabs toward their own weapons.

The chatter-gun tracked onto Iron Mike Cappolini and shredded the elbow of his gun arm just as his revolver was clearing leather. The .38 kept moving, flying from the grasp of suddenly nerveless fingers to shatter the painted glass wall of the office. Meanwhile the firetrack of death swept on, seeking and finding vital matter. Iron Mike's throat exploded in twin crimson geysers; the big guy twisted to his knees and flopped face down into his own blood.

Jack the Bartender Avanti managed to jerk off two panicky shots toward that furiously blazing muzzle of death as he sprinted for the rear door. Then Death overtook him and pummeled him into a twisting, sliding heap at the back wall.

Collectors John Brunelli and Ham Magliocci, noted and feared throughout South Philly for their uninhibited pursuit of payday loan "vigorish", received their final collections as they scampered for cover behind the wooden desk stacked with the fruits of their toil. Brunelli's outflung arm raked the desk clean as he oozed across it; the collectors and the collected shared a common heap within the pool of blood that quickly marked the end of vigorish.

Death had "come fearful quick" to Cappy's Liberty Garage—so quickly, in fact, that a mechanic and a customer standing just beyond that shattered glass wall were still frozen into shocked statues when the chattering knell ceased and quiet descended.

Gawking at the carnage through the broken wall, both men reacted with swiftly raising hands as the tall figure in executioner black turned calm attention upon them.

These two would later aver that the sight of Death Alive and Looking was even more unnerving than the sudden presence of Death Eternal Still. It was clad in black tight-fitting combat garb —belts crisscrossing the chest, another encircling the waist, "guns and stuff hanging from them", the machine pistol suspended from a cord about the shoulders, eyes of bluest ice regarding them from an expressionless face of chiseled steel.

The muzzle of the chatter-gun dropped. The tall man's hand moved in an almost imperceptible flick of motion. A small metallic object flew through the shattered wall and clattered to the cement floor at the men's feet.

"That's for Don Stefano," a cool voice informed them. "Tell him. It's over. Tell him."

And then the tall apparition in black was gone, fading quickly into the shadows at the rear wall.

Perhaps ten seconds had elapsed since the first rattling burst of automatic weapons fire.

The two spectators to the awesome event did not move until they heard the door open and close; then the customer took a staggering step backwards and exclaimed in an awed whisper, "Christ—did you *see* that guy!"

The mechanic knelt to extend a shaking hand toward the metallic object on the floor. He picked it up, examined it, and released a hissing sigh.

"Yeah. That's what it is," he declared with a quiet rush of breath.

"What? What is it?"

"A marksman's medal. The Brotherly Love Outfit is in for it now."

"You saying that was Mack Bolan, the guy they call *the Executioner?*" the other man said, awed. He bent forward for a closer look at the medal. "You saying this place is a *Mafia front?*"

"It *was*," the mechanic replied quietly, peering

17

toward Death in the next room. "But . . . like the guy said . . . it's over now."

Not quite.

Mack Bolan knew better.

The Panic in Philly had only just begun.

POLICE BUSINESS
**RESTRICTED COMMUNIQUE**
SCRAMBLE CIRCUIT AUTHY #PH105
FROM PHILA PD 141025L
TO H BROGNOLA/USDOJ/WASHDC
**URGENT**
BT
BOLAN STRUCK THIS CITY APPROX 0900
THIS DATE. MACHINE-GUNNED LOAN
RACKETEER MICHAEL J CAPPOLINI
AND FOUR UNDERLINGS. LOCAL
INFORMANTS REPORT MASSIVE
MOVEMENTS ORGCRIME TRIGGERMEN.
REQUEST ALL FEDERAL ASSISTANCE
POSSIBLE.
BT
DOUGHERTY PHILA SENDS
EOM

## Chapter 2/   Gradigghia

In a western Massachusetts city several hundred miles removed from the developments at Philadelphia, the number two man in that city's local Mafia arm paced restlessly about his modest headquarters in a downtown office building.

He was a handsome man in his early thirties, medium height and build, with darkly glinting eyes which could switch in a flash from affable warmth to frosty speculation.

His name was Turrin; sometimes he was referred to but never directly addressed as Leo the Pussy.

Leo Turrin was a blood nephew of the late Sergio Frenchi, the boss of Western Massachusetts until his organization committed the blunder of the century—it was the Frenchi "family" which had figured in the birth of Mack Bolan's home-front war against the mob.

Uncle Sergio had died during that initial skirmish and his family had fallen into almost total disarray. Leo the Pussy had proved a strong rallying point for the reconstitution of that vital Mafia arm and he had risen considerably in stature in the new organization.

Like Bolan, Turrin was a Vietnam veteran. Prior to his army service, he had resisted the tantalizing pull of Uncle Sergio and his assurances of easy money and practically unlimited power.

Though he had grown up in its shadow, Leo had forever despised the Mafia and all that it stood for. With Vietnam behind him, however—and a resultant new maturity—Turrin "came in" with the Frenchi family, but he brought the entire federal government in with him.

That "penetration" had developed into the most successful undercover police operation ever attempted against the mob. With his favored position as blood relative to the aging *Capo*, Turrin's rise to importance in the Pittsfield arm was almost automatic. He had balanced upon the edge of that knife for more than five years, had become a *Caporegime* under Frenchi, and was beginning to attain national stature when Bolan the Bold came along.

The blitz artist had hit Uncle Sergio's little kingdom with thunder and lightning, damn near dislodging Turrin himself in the process. Only the last-minute revelation of Turrin's true role had saved him from Bolan's vengeance. From the rubble, though, the undercover cop had built for himself an even stronger position and considerable prestige in the national reaches of the syndicate.

He had also salvaged from those ruins the beginning of a great, if terribly hazardous, friendship with Mack Bolan.

Turrin personally considered himself as neither fish nor fowl. His active friendship with Bolan presented no conflict of duties in his own mind. He was a cop . . . but not really. He was a *Mafioso* . . . but not really. The only *real* thing he had found during five years of carefully manufactured deceit was the continuing relationship with the man whom both the law and the mob considered public enemy number one. To Turrin's mind, Mack Bolan was the greatest human being alive. He wasn't perfect, no—not even infallible—but still the by God *greatest* human being Turrin had ever encountered.

A man like Bolan did not happen to the world every day, nor even in every age or epoch. The Bolans of the world came few and far between. You could count them on humanity's ten fingers, all the ones who had ever been.

And Leo Turrin worried a lot about Mack Bolan.

Perhaps no one, not Bolan himself, understood better than Leo Turrin the staggering array of forces pitted against the guy's survival. Turrin was in a position to view both sides of the guy's personal gauntlet, the cops as well as the mob . . . and yeah, he had good reason for worry. He'd done a lot of pacing the past few days, waiting, wondering when the claws of the pincers would close around the world's best answer to *La Cosa Nostra*.

And so it was on that brooding Spring afternoon when the call finally came.

Turrin's personal shadow, a goon called Hot Stuff Ribiello, scooped up the phone and muttered into it. "Yeah. I dunno, just a minute." He caught Turrin's expressionless eye and announced, "Long distance, collect. For you, boss. Guy named La-Mancha. You wanta accept?"

The underboss of Pittsfield coolly replied, "I don't know no LaMancha."

22

"He don't know no LaMancha," Ribiello relayed to the operator. "Tell the guy to get lost."

"Tell him to spend his own damn nickle," Turrin instructed boredly.

"He should spend his own nickles," the goon dutifully relayed. He laughed and hung up. "Some of these boys really got their nerve. I never made a collect call in my whole life even."

"Good for you," Turrin growled. He rubbed the back of his neck, then moved the hand around to massage the throat. "Hell," he told the bodyguard, "I got to get some air. I'm going out to smell some sunshine."

Turrin started for the door. Rubiello trudged along behind.

"Not you," Turrin growled. "Stay put. I'm expecting Jake to call. Get the number where he's at and I'll call 'im back."

"Don't stand on no street corners," the bodyguard suggested, as he gladly returned to the comfort of his chair.

Turrin grunted and ambled into the hallway. He lit a cigarette and displayed outward patience as he waited for the elevator. In the lobby he chatted for a moment with the girl at the newsstand, then drifted out the back way and across the parking lot, pausing now and then to sniff the air and flex his shoulders at the sun.

Precisely five minutes after rejection of the collect call from LaMancha, Turrin stepped into a public phone booth a block and a half from his office building, just in time to answer the first ring.

23

"Yeah, dammit, what's been keeping you?" he asked without preamble.

A cool chuckle drifted through the instrument and a pleasantly modulated voice informed him, "Just got your broadcast twenty minutes ago. What's the flap?"

"The flap, buddy, is your bloody ass," Turrin growled. "Everybody wants it, and in that condition. I was hoping you'd call before—"

"Too late," reported the real live Man from LaMancha, Mack Bolan.

"Yeah, I know, I heard it," Turrin said gloomily. "Of all places, Sarge, why *Philly?* Why not Kansas City or Hot Springs, why not Dallas or Phoenix or—hell, even St. Louis or Detroit? Philly is where the big guns are mobbing up, Philly's the place—"

"You know why I'm here, Leo."

"Yeah, yeah. I guess it figures."

"Did you have something specific in mind, Mother, or did you just want to say good-bye?"

"Specific, yeah," Turrin growled. "I'd say that. Message from your buddy in Washington. He suggests quote take a vacation unquote."

"Brognola, eh?"

"Yeh. He's walking a tightrope, you know. Officially he's running the entire national *Get Bolan* show. Unofficially his guts turn over every time he thinks about it. But you know Hal. The job is the job."

"Wouldn't have it any other way," Bolan murmured. He sighed. Turrin heard the click of a cigarette lighter and a slow, hissing exhalation. "Sounds like I'm back in season."

"Worse yet. The heat is on—very. Some congressional subcommittee is stoking the boiler. Hal thinks it'd be a good time for you to catch some R&R. He says Argentina is beautiful this time of year."

The chuckle from the other end of the connection was downright icy. "Lousy hunting down there, Leo."

"Yeah." The number two man of Pittsfield shook away a spinal shiver. "Well, listen . . ."

A moment later, Bolan replied, "I'm listening."

"I wouldn't try Philly right now. Don Stefano has been expecting you. The word I hear, he's imported a private army just to wait for your head to show. I think—"

"Imported from where?"

"The old country. Sicily. Very mean—"

"*Gradigghia*," Bolan muttered.

"That's the word. And I'll give you another, buddy. *Malacarni*. It means a very bold dude, capable of anything. These old-country *gradigghia,* the Sicilian Mafia gangs, are composed entirely of people like that. They are very mean boys."

"So I hear," Bolan commented. "How are they getting them in?"

"Canada's the usual route. The New York bosses started it. I hear now that Augie Marinello is running a regular body shop in imported guns. And old Stefano Angeletti isn't letting any grass grow under his feet. He's got a—"

"They running out of native talent?"

"You should know," Turrin replied soberly. "Anyway, Don Stefano has this standing army of

25

imported torpedoes. And they're not standing there just to shade his tired old head from the sun."

"Thanks, Leo. I'll keep that in mind. Well. . ."

"Hold it, don't hand up yet. Listen. This isn't from Brognola. This is from me. Don Stefano's army isn't the only one you have to worry about. They're bringing in cops from all around. City cops, county cops, state cops, federal cops. I've been watching the movements. They mean to get your ass this time, buddy."

Bolan's voice had gone totally sober and just a shade fainter. "Nobody lives forever, Leo. I have to fight it where it lays."

"Well, you've picked the right lay this time."

"That's the idea, isn't it?"

"Yeah," Turrin agreed, sighing. "I guess that's what you're all about, windmill slayer. Okay. It's your war. I just wanted you to know what it is you're walking into this time."

"Thanks. While you're here, give me something else."

"Like what?"

"A weakness."

"Well. . ." Turrin was thinking about it. "The kid, I guess. Stefano's son, Frank Angeletti. The old man has been grooming Frankie for the keys to the kingdom. But nobody really likes the choice."

"Kid's not rotten enough, eh?" Bolan said.

Turrin laughed feebly. "He's not what you'd call a strong man. He's not *Capo* material, Sarge."

Bolan replied, "Okay, I'll look into that. How about the girl?"

"Sometimes," Turrin said, "I wonder who is feeding whom in this crazy interchange of ours. I'll bet you know Stefano Angeletti's whole family more intimately than he does."

The cold chuckle sounded again. "What about her, Leo?"

"I'll just say this, Sarge. If the Mafia outfits were not full of male chauvinist pigs, old Stefano would do a lot better to hand over his keys to his daughter, not his son. She's everything the old man would like for Frankie to be, which *he* definitely is not."

"Okay. That checks with my reading. Thanks, Leo. Uh, just one more item."

Turrin knew what the "one more item" was. Bolan always sounded a bit embarrassed to inquire about his kid brother, Johnny, and the girl he'd left behind under Leo's protection, faithful Val.

"They're fine," he replied. "They—"

"Okay, great, don't tell me anything else. Our time is up, anyway. Thanks, Leo. I couldn't hack it without you."

"Bullshit," Turrin replied mildly.

And then there was nothing but the hum of the broken connection.

Turrin sighed, hung up, moved out into the warming sun, and allowed the shivers to play with his backbone.

The guy couldn't keep it going forever, God knew.

Very probably he would not keep it going even

27

through Philly. Not with those odds—the cops, all those cops—the *gradigghia.* . .

*Shit!*

Leo the Pussy squared his shoulders in a movement of self-reassurance and strode quickly toward his office.

One thing those Angeletti *gradigghia* had better understand, for damn sure.

Mack Bolan was one hell of a superior *malacarni* himself.

## Chapter 3 / *The Challenge*

Sure, Bolan had known about the importation of old-country *gradigghia* to bolster the U.S. Mafia's sagging hard-arms.

It had been an inevitable development.

Guys like Capone, Luciano, and Anastasia had been products of their times—the hard old days of the American boom-and-bust era when the Italian-Americans, as an ethnic group, were in the cellar of American society—when a hungry, angry young man had to simply grab what he wanted and to hell with the consequences.

Times had changed.

Big city ghettoes were now peopled by Blacks, Puerto Ricans, and a general hodgepodge of have-nots of all races and national origins.

The Irish gangs were gone.

The Italian gangs were all but gone.

The Jew boys were gone.

The Blacks and those others who were left could not put it together—not like the Lucianos and the Lanskys and the Schulzes, the Legs Diamonds and the Mad Dog Colls. One reason they couldn't put it together was because the American crime scene had become so institutionalized—incorporated, almost—finely organized. The guys at the top of the pyramid were the survivors and the heirs of those hard, early days when "welfare" meant a pick and shovel and the Italians were the meanest, the quickest, and the most utterly determined to escape those selfsame picks and shovels and pushbrooms.

Those same guys continued to dominate the organized crime territories of America.

But they were getting old.

And those who were coming up behind them were products of far different times. They didn't have the hunger, the desperation, the sheer driving determination to survive and excel in a dog-eat-dog world.

The American Mafia had grown "soft"—in comparison with the old days, at any rate.

Success had spoiled Johnny Matthew.

He wanted it safe, now. He wanted it comfortable. He wanted to *have* without *risking*, to *keep* without *struggling*, to *succeed* without *trying*.

So he hired Blacks and Puerto Ricans and other hungry young men to do his dirty work.

And it simply wasn't working out. The mob was losing its sense of solidarity in brotherhood—and with that loss went the teeth, the muscle, and the heart of the organization. Nickle-and-dime guys simply didn't give a shit about *omertà*, family fealty, discipline.

The thing that had made Johnny Matthew the lord of his jungle was his ferocity of spirit, his unwatered orneriness, his instinctive leap to violence.

And those "attributes" were disappearing from the latter-day American *Mafioso*.

A man did not become a *Capo* because he was *loved* by those he ruled. He was *Capo* because he was the meanest and the most feared. It was as simple as that.

Of course, there were still plenty of the mean ones around. Bolan could certainly attest to that. But he himself had removed quite a few of those from circulation. The federal strike forces had put away a few more. These actions, coupled with the normal attrition through aging and interfamily violence, were combining to put the handwriting on the wall for all who had eyes to see. So, sure, it was no surprise to Bolan to learn that "the organization" was trekking to the old country for an infusion of hot new blood into their declining empire.

It was still "the hard old days" in Sicily.

The rugged country villages and harsh ghetto streets of the urban centers where *Onorata Società*— the Mafia—was born could provide virtually bottomless pools of *malacarni* manpower; new blood which was still immersed in the old ways, subject to disciplines of *omertà*—honored silence—and unquestioning loyalty to the chief.

There had been a time, and not too long ago, when foreign-born lower-echelon *Mafiosi* had been treated contemptuously by the native Americans. They'd been referred to as "greasers" and "mustache Petes" and other uncomplimentary tags.

Not now.

The new immigrants were being accorded considerable respect, even from those whom they had come to replace. Augie Marinello, the New York superboss, had started the trend toward imported hoods, bringing over an occasional one or two for specific tasks at hand, then retaining and absorbing them into the established ranks.

They had proven to be nerveless assassins as well as loyal servants of the brotherhood.

So old man Angeletti had gone Marinello one better. He was bringing in entire *gradigghia,* or gangs, in an awesome buildup of muscle such as had not been attempted since the old Castellam-marese wars.

According to Bolan's intelligence, Don Stefano intended to use the new cadre not only for his own security but as an eventual base of power for his son, Frank Angeletti, who would soon be succeeding the old man as boss of Philadelphia.

It was, to Bolan, an ominous development in his war. Until recently there had been a gleam of light at the end of the tunnel; he had begun to see the possibility of victory in this impossible damn war. But if the *Capi* could draw upon an unlimited reserve of manpower, then, yeah, the whole thing was beginning to look hopeless again.

So Bolan had come to Philadelphia to face this new enemy, to test them, and—if possible—to turn them back.

He had to discourage the whole idea of imported gunners. If he could not convince the American *Capi* that they'd placed their chips on the wrong numbers, then he at least had to put the fear of something else into the Sicilians.

Those guys had come from withered pastures to what must have seemed like lush new fields. They'd had everything to gain and very little to lose by venturing into the U.S.

Bolan would have to give them something to lose.

It was precisely why he had come to Philadelphia —to bring war, death, fear, panic. Especially death.

The Executioner had come to Philly to rout the foreign armies.

So maybe he could and maybe he couldn't.

Maybe Leo was right and he didn't stand a chance against the Philadelphia defenses. But he had to try. He had to.

Following the brief telephone contact with Leo Turrin, Bolan returned directly to his latest version of *the warwagon*.

It was a late-model Chevy panel truck, closely resembling a telephone company service vehicle. Actually the Chevy was a mobile combat command post and arsenal. In there was everything he would need to wage war against the Brotherly Love Outfit and its outriders.

Over his black combat outfit he had donned loose-fitting coveralls similar to those worn by telephone linemen.

He had located the main enemy force. He had served notice of his presence and had delivered his declaration of war.

Two days of painstaking recon and combat planning had shown him the most likely approach to this new enemy.

Nothing remained now but to do it.

It was time. It was time to tell the *gradigghia* that they had ventured into hell's pastures.

It was time for the first big Philly hit.

## Chapter 4 / *Combat Zone*

He had been watching them closely for three hours, inspecting every movement, taking mental note of every coming and going, counting their numbers, identifying each one by size or shape or by peculiarities of walk and posture.

Among the many he had tagged were Big Swagger and Little Swagger, a couple of Palermo street types who must have once been influenced by an American gangster movie. They looked like very dangerous boys, movie-struck or not.

There was Joe the Ox, a big guy with barrel chest, massive shoulders and spindly legs who walked as though the oversized torso was continually straining against a heavy load—the guy must have pulled many a plow through the rocky soil of Sicily. Bolan made a mental note to remain well out of reach of the big animal. He looked like a spine crusher.

Then there was the sharp dresser who stood around a lot and watched the others, his arms folded across his chest, speaking to none, every so often brushing the back of his hand against a bulge near his heart as though to reassure himself that the hardware was still there. Bolan tagged him Shotgun Pete and marked him as an early target.

Several times during the surveillance old man Angeletti put in an appearance in the little court-yard just outside the main building for an arm-waving, emotional conversation with one or more of these principals, each of whom was obviously a crew leader or whatever they called themselves in the *gradigghia*.

Once Bolan caught a glimpse of Frank Angeletti, the Don's shrinking heir-apparent, well flanked by a retinue of alert bodyguards. Once also he thought he saw a female face peering through an upstairs window but the sun angle was bad on that side and he couldn't be positive of the identification.

He could be certain of one thing, however. They were setting their defenses in an apparent anticipation of a night attack. Don Stefano had beat it out there almost the moment he'd received word of the Liberty Garage strike. The preparations for an Executioner visit had been going on at a feverish pace ever since. They'd buried almost as much wire as Bolan had strung over their heads; they were putting in cute little electric-eye floodlight traps, digging foxholes and positioning fire teams.

Bolan did not intend to play that hand. He had been up and down every telephone pole in the neighborhood, stringing dummy wire as he went, studying the layout inside those walls from every available angle and planning his own strike his own way.

And this, he had decided, would have to be a daylight hit.

It was in Northwest Philadelphia—out beyond Germantown, in the upper Fairmount Park area—that Bolan had decided to issue his first dose of blitzkrieg to Papa Angeletti. It was a quiet neighborhood of parkland, hospitals, social institutions, schools, and private clubs of various types.

The combat zone itself had once been the site of a small college, about a four-acre plot of land abutting the park and set off by a crumbling eighteenth century wall of fieldstone. The original building remained, a vine-covered brick structure of two stories, rather small and unpretentious in this age of super-architecture. Surrounding it were a collection of ten bungalow-style smaller buildings. These had obviously been built in more recent times, with no apparent attempt to gracefully bridge the centuries between the architectural styles.

The college itself had long ago ceased to exist. Somewhere around the beginning of the twentieth century the site had become the home of a local millionnaire who had renovated and modernized the interior facilities. Little else had been done to the old building until the early 1950's when it once again became a seat of learning. The original classrooms were restored at that time, the bungalows added, and the "Fairmount School for Special Children" came into being.

The new school had catered to handicapped children of well-to-do families, providing resident education and medical services "in a homelike atmosphere"—this latter claim being attested to by the new bungalow-style dormitories, each of which could house eight to ten children in a family environment. Each bungalow featured a kitchen, dining room, recreation room, a large formal living room and five double bedrooms.

Stefano Angeletti had picked up the property in

1965—"at a price they couldn't refuse"—and turned it over to son Frank in a bid to "put some legs under the boy".

The idea had been to create the classiest whorehouse in the East, catering exclusively to carefully selected VIP's in business, labor, and political circles. The old building had been lavishly renovated, walls removed, marble floors and bubbling fountains installed, and a veritable "Caesar's Palace" created.

The finished product was rumored to have cost the Don "more than a million bucks". Untold thousands more went into a refurbishing of the ten bungalow units, in which smaller "private parties" could be lavishly staged in satisfaction of virtually any offbeat sexual appetite.

The original idea had been Frank's. Don Stefano had put up the money, the influence, and the contacts to get the new club into operation. Frank had brainstormed the renovation and flapped about with the interior decorators. He had also personally recruited each of the dazzlingly beautiful hostesses and, as the story goes, "bed-tested every damn one of 'em."

At the height of its popularity, the "Emperor's Key" private club was booking parties and business conventions from throughout the country. According to a classified FBI report, the club numbered in its membership an impressive list of state and federal bureaucrats and elected officials.

These had been Frank Angeletti's most glorious days, a brief era when he had rubbed shoulders with some of the most powerful men in the nation.

The younger Angeletti had been operating beyond his depth, however, and the bright new bubble of success blew up in his face early in the second year of operation.

The "fall" had been typical of Frank's many other aborted ventures.

Without first consulting his father or anyone else, Frank the Kid had taken it upon himself to "clout" a local federal judge by adding him to the Emperor's secret membership roles and sending him his own personally monogrammed key with an invitation to attend the premiere performance of a new "very special live show in our Theatre-in-the-Round."

The invitation, as it turned out, was a sad error in judgment. Perhaps it had never occurred to Frank that not every man would feel honored by a VIP membership in the classiest whorehouse in the East, nor even recognize the honor when it descended upon him.

The unsuspecting judge turned out for the event, all right, but with his wife and daughter in tow. The flustered doorman didn't quite know how to handle the situation and he couldn't locate Frank the Kid for advice.

The judge and his ladies were eventually seated in the Roman Gardens on a waterbed couch surrounded by tables of wines and fresh fruits just as the curtain was going up on "Sinbed the Great and his Harem of Bedspring Acrobats".

Sinbed was the only male in the troupe of ten but it immediately became evident that he was the

38

only male needed and also the best acrobat in the bunch.

The judge and his ladies beat a frantic retreat just as Sinbed the Great was demonstrating his unique ability to service nine moaning lovelies simultaneously.

Thirty minutes later the joint was raided by a flying squad of county vice agents, and not even Papa Angeletti could salvage anything of lasting value from that disaster, even though he did manage to quiet the thing and keep most of the big-name guests off of the official police blotter.

The Emperor's Key club disintegrated virtually overnight. Frank the Kid, a mere thirty-two years of age at the time, went on to bigger and better disasters. Papa Angeletti sighed and alibied, and kept hoping that some day "the kid" would find some legs under him.

From that time until very recently, the property in Northwest Philly had been in mothballs.

Now it was a camp for Don Stefano's foreign recruits. They were billeted five to a house with all ten bungalows occupied. The old building was being used, once again, as some sort of school. It figured. Most of the guys spoke no English. If they were to avoid problems over their illegal entry, they would need some understanding of the language. They also would need carefully constructed new identities. The Don was the sort to take care of little details like that. Sure. He was sending those dudes to school. For some of them, it was for the first time in their lives.

Bolan was satisfied now that he had their numbers and their defensive layout. The sun was dropping into the west and the shadows were growing long across the grounds of the *gradigghia* encampment.

He tied off the last of his dummy cable and descended the final pole of his grid. By no coincidence, it was placed directly across the street from the joint's main gate.

He crossed over and, as he removed the climbing spikes from his ankles, struck up a one-sided conversation with one of the troops, a bright-eyed guy of about twenty-five who was lounging about just inside the gate and trying his best not to look like a sentry.

Bolan wagged his head toward the pole he had just abandoned and told the guy, "Warm day for winter, eh? Guess it'll snow tonight."

It was Spring. The sky was clear and unruffled. The temperature was hovering near the seventy mark.

But the guy smiled, jerked his head in a reply somewhere between yes and no, and spread his arms.

Bolan smiled back, said, "Hell, I guess. You're a dumb shit, you know that? I think I'll kick your teeth out."

The guy kept on smiling. He said, "That's what I say," with beautiful articulation, showed Bolan gleaming teeth, rubbed his chest, and ambled away.

The guy was no dumb shit. He'd handled it beautifully, reading Bolan's face instead of his words, and the response would have been perfect for most small-talk.

But he obviously had understood not a word.

And there were *fifty* more just like that dude inside those walls.

The combat freeze was seeping into Bolan's chest, trying its best to arrest the heartbeat and paralyze the lungs.

It was going to be a mean mother this time.

The Executioner returned to the warwagon and stripped off the coveralls, then began field-checking his weapons.

A daylight strike.

Fifty very mean dudes who had everything to gain and nothing to lose.

This one would have to be played directly on the numbers.

There would be no room whatever for the slightest fumbling or miscalculation. There would be room only for death—either his or his enemies.

Bolan the Bastard meant to make it *them*. Or die trying.

*I'm going in to meet the* gradigghia. *This isn't just a wild-ass charge to prove who's the meanest. It's probably the most crucial maneuver of my war. It may even decide who'll be running this country for the next few years.*

—a page from Mack Bolan's journal

He dropped in over the wall, coming from the street side in full combat regalia, landing behind a bungalow and almost directly over one of the hastily dug defenses.

A head popped from the foxhole, the guy's mouth opening to scream out the alarm. There was nothing in his hands but a small shovel.

The silent Beretta phutted once and the cry of alarm was buttoned into collapsing jaws, choked, drowned and reduced to a gushing whimper. Black death moved swiftly on.

He'd launched the assault at the best possible moment, when most of the troops were inside the old building getting stoked up on a hasty meal and a last-minute combat briefing.

The outside guard numbered less than ten, with just about all of these engaged in the final preparations for the coming night.

He carried the .44 AutoMag flesh-shredder strapped to his right hip, the whispering Beretta in snap-draw leather beneath his left arm, the little auto chatter-pistol dangling at waist level from a shoulder cord.

Fragmentation grenades and incendiaries were clipped to his belts. Smokesticks occupied the slit-pockets below his knees. Coils of doughlike plastic explosives were wrapped about his neck.

A one-man assault force had to also be a pack mule. In a show like this, he got but one jump-off and he had to have it all together the first time around.

Bolan had it all together.

Thirty seconds inside the walls he already had plastic "goop" clinging to four of the bungalows, with ninety-second fuses attached and counting down.

By thirty-five numbers past jump-off he was moving between the two central bungalows. At that same moment Shotgun Pete came striding out of the courtyard at the side of the main building, a sandwich in his left hand, the right hand enjoying the subconscious back-of-the-hand stroking of concealed hardware.

The guy gaped in mid-bite, then threw the sandwich over his shoulder and broke buttons getting the coat open as he spun into the confrontation with advancing death.

The range was about fifty yards. Bolan instinctively went for the heavy piece, the AutoMag arcing up and exploding into the hair-trigger response even before reaching full extension.

Shotgun Pete's spinning motion was arrested as though he'd run into some invisible wall and he died at thirty-nine numbers, the itchy right hand mutilated by a big 240-grain bullet that blasted on through and ripped the heart right out of the guy.

The roaring report of the .44 brought immediate response from several quarters.

Not a spare number was available to the tall grim man in black, however. He ignored the angry yapping of the several handguns which were challenging him, and continued the charge.

At thirty yards out he baseballed a fragmentation grenade through the big window at the front of the joint, following immediately with an incendiary blast. The quick one-two punch jarred the old building, sending flames and smoke huffing through the shattered window.

At forty-seven numbers he turned the chatter-pistol into a retort to the growing menace of the handgun defenses, forcing two guys on his right flank to dive for cover behind a bungalow and catching a *malacarni* on his left who was sprinting in for closer range with a figure-eight burst that removed him from the range utterly and forever.

Mixed somewhere into those numbers a shotgun barrel emerged from an upstairs window of the old building, and Bolan found himself moving through an atmosphere suddenly thickened with spraying buckshot.

Luckily the person behind the gun had not bothered with choke-settings; the few pellets which found target were insufficient to the task at hand.

Bolan shrugged away the stinging strikes, emptying his clip in a blazing sweep of the four windows facing him up there. The shotgun clattered to the courtyard, accompanied by a rain of shattered glass and nothing else—but there was no more static from the upper level.

It was seventy numbers into the strike. The AutoMag was effectively persuading a noisily alarmed hard force to remain with the burning building when Bolan suddenly broke off the attack and began his withdrawal along the reverse course, back between the bungalows and along the wall to the precise point where he had entered.

A hot pursuit was materializing behind him, with guys pouring in from everywhere. On top of that, a familiar figure was on his knees and peering into a foxhole directly in Bolan's path.

At eighty-five and counting, he sent a 240-grain magnum bonecrusher exploding into the forehead of Big Swagger as the latter raised startled eyes from an inspection of Bolan's first victim of the strike; then Bolan was over the wall and crouching behind it, eyes on the GP Quartz at his wrist.

Silently his lips formed the word "ninety" as right on the numbers the four bungalows he'd gooped for doomsday found the end of their ninety-second fuses and lifted themselves into oblivion —a goodly number of *malacarni,* Bolan presumed, tagging along in a sudden departure from hot pursuit.

He sheathed the AutoMag, crossed casually to the warwagon, and unhurriedly drove away from there.

At the intersection with Germantown Avenue, he met and yielded to a screaming procession of fire-fighting equipment and police vehicles. When they were all safely by and tearing along Bolan's backtrack, he again consulted his wristwatch, blotted a spot of blood from his cheek, and muttered, "Bingo, right on the numbers."

From Bolan's journal:
*I have met the enemy and I guess they're mine. But let's not get too cocky about it. Ten more seconds in there and I'd have been a dead dude. And it's not ended yet.*

No, the Philadelphia hit had not ended yet, nor had it even found a pause. Already the Executioner was racing toward the next round with the Angeletti *Mafiosi.*

Chapter 6/ *Without Numbers*

Stefano Angeletti had been seated at the small dining table with his son Frank and two of his lieutenants, Carmine Drasco from South Philly and Jules Sticatta from downtown, when the fireworks started.

On the wall above the table hung a large, hand-painted sign in a foreign language which, translated, urged everyone within sight of it to:

SPEAK AMERICAN
THINK AMERICAN
BE AMERICAN

The soldiers who were seated at the long table just opposite were obviously being intimidated by the instructions. They were eating in absolute silence, devouring stacks of roast beef sandwiches and washing them down with cheap wine as the *Capi* at the small table went through their final review of the strategy for the night.

Only a moment earlier, Frank Angeletti had caught the eye of one of the Sicilian crew bosses and, breaking his own rule, growled a command in the old tongue: *"Scrusci-scrusci."*

Literally translated, the phrase meant "squeaky shoes" but in old-country Mafia slang it referred to a reliable scout, one who could be counted upon to recon a dangerous situation.

The man got up and went out, taking his sandwich with him.

Immediately thereafter the hell began, with a single rolling boom from a high-powered firearm.

Frank the Kid froze with his wine glass halfway to his lips, eyes glazing as they sought reassurance from the others at the table.

Papa Angeletti was raised off his chair and stared speculatively toward the front of the house.

A wave of quiet exclamations was surging along the long table of soldiers.

Then the building shook and a great explosion banged open the door at the front of the room, sending in whoofing smoke and powdered plaster.

Before anyone could react to that unsettling development, angrily popping sparks of white-hot chemicals sizzled through the opening and sent the soldiers scattering in all directions from their dining table.

As fast as that, the place was a disaster area—the table overturned, chairs scattered about and excited men scampering to escape the popping incendiaries.

Don Stefano was screaming, "Awright, that's *it!* Get out there, *out* there!"

One of Frank the Kid's foreign bodyguards lurched through the blown door at that very moment, spraying blood from multiple punctures, and ablaze from head to foot. The guy sent a pleading look to the men at the small table, then fell forward into their midst.

Jules Sticatta tried to wrap the burning man in the tablecloth but the cloth itself ignited, then Sticatta's own clothing began to flame.

Don Stefano and the other lieutenant went to

48

Sticatta's aid while Frank watched in agape horror, stunned by the sickening odor of burnt flesh.

Meanwhile the whole encampment had come alive with the furious crackling of gunshots, joined quickly after the bomb or whatever by the electrifying chatter of a machine gun.

Frank could hear people screaming around outside there, yelling urgent cries and instructions in the old tongue. The inside soldiers were piling up at the patio doors, trying to get a look at what they might be running into before they quit the temporary safety of the dining room.

Frank screamed at them, " '*ncarugnuti,* (shirkers, or cowards) *va! va!* (get out there!) "

The *ba-loom* of a shotgun overhead partially drowned out the emotional command, but the patio door opened and a couple of the Sicilians went scrambling outside, only to return quickly in a sudden shower of glass from the windows above them.

And then Frank the Kid got a clear, unobstructed look at the big cool bastard outside, the bastard in black, standing right out in the open and daring them to come get him, blasting away at that crowd in the doorway with a big silver pistol, big heavy booms like that first one sending fantastically whistling slugs hurtling through those glass doors and splattering everything they touched.

Frank found himself on the floor, with the rest of them, though still shouting that they go out there and *get* that bastard, *get him!*

Something turned his attention momentarily to the stairway and he later recalled seeing his sister Philippa standing there on the bottom step, leaning against the wall and clasping a bleeding hand to her bosom. Their eyes met and she stammered, "I—I hit him, I know I did, but h—he didn't go down."

More urgent considerations were demanding his attention, however, and he took only passing notice of his sister who refused to act like a woman.

The *malacarni* had apparently found their pride, or something, and they were scrambling out windows and doors and racing into that open combat zone. Frank leapt to his feet and shouted them on, then turned back to see about his father.

It had all come so damned *fast*.

The whole place was shooting flames.

Carmine Drasco was standing at a window overlooking the carport and yelling for somebody to bring the cars around.

Jules Sticatta was stumbling around in his underwear, groaning with pain and being assisted by Don Stefano. Poor Jules was in bad shape; a single glance was all it took to know that.

They'd *all* be in a similar spot if they didn't do something quick, that much was also evident.

"What're we doing?" Frank yelled at his father.

"Getting outta here!" the elder Angeletti yelled back. "You go tell those boys of yours, they scatter before the *zaffa* (police) come. You tell 'em!"

Frank swallowed hard, got his legs under him, and ventured outside. By some miracle he lucked onto one of the crew bosses right outside the door and passed the instruction; then he went back to help Papa get Jules Sticatta to the car.

The other explosions came as they were hurrying into the vehicles, four big blasts that shook the air, sending instant flames rolling skyward, and Carmine Drasco gasped, "Oh, Jesus, I just saw a bunch of boys run right *into* that!"

But there was no time to mourn the dying. The big limousine leapt forward and sped across the lawn toward the escape gate at the rear, the tricky secret exit which Frank himself had dreamed up for his Emperor's Key clientele.

Carmine's personal wheelman was driving. Drasco himself and his longtime bodyguard were also up front. Stefano and the painfully injured Jules Sticatta were in the back. Frank and Philippa sat tensely on the jumpseats. A backup car of hardmen was right on their rear bumper.

Frank looked back upon the scene of combat as they cleared the gate and shot up the back road. His beautiful fucking joint was wreathed in flames, burning . . . burning to the fucking ground.

"So fast," Frank groaned. "It happened so fast."

"How'd he do it?" Drasco's bodyguard muttered, scowling into the rear-view mirror. "In broad daylight. How'd the guy *do* it?"

Philippa was pressing a bloodsoaked handkerchief against a bullet graze on the back of her hand. She was scared—sure—like the rest of them . . . but more than that, she was stunned, really out of it. "I hit him," she was whispering. ". . . I know I hit him."

"I saw the guy," Frank announced. "Plain as day, big as a mountain, I saw him."

"Big deal," somebody up front growled in a half-audible sneer. "He *saw* him."

"Shut up!" Papa Angeletti roared from the back seat. "All of you just *shut up!* Maybe we ain't out of it yet!"

Frank shivered and glanced over his shoulder for a comforting peek at the loaded crew wagon behind them. Even Don Stefano, the unshakable, the unflappable—even he was scared. When Papa yelled and talked like the streets, yeah . . . Frank the Kid knew, the old man was shook and flapping.

The two-car caravan screeched around a corner, edging out a green panel truck which was angling into that same crossroads. The truck gave them plenty of room—then they ignored the warning sirens and also beat a procession of fire trucks into the intersection at Germantown Avenue. When they were leveled out and eating pavement toward home, the wheelman lifted his gaze into the rearview to watch the last of the emergency vehicles disappear.

"Bet I know where they're headed," he commented quietly.

"Already?" Frank asked under his breath.

How could everything be happening so fast? How could those fire trucks already be. . . ?

He sighed and declared aloud, "I think we got ourselves a mess."

"You think, you think," the Don grumbled. "Listen, and you mark me what I'm saying! I gonna get his *head!* I gonna get that wise guy's *head* and I gonna make me a *boccie ball* outta it! You mark me!"

Frank the Kid was marking him.

But he was still shivering in his hundred-dollar

boots . . . and with no legs, no legs at all, under him.

Frank Angeletti would have shivered even harder if he'd known about the green panel truck which was laying off their tails by about a cool city block and the ice-eyed man in black who, with cold singleness of purpose, was tracking the hit to the next zone of combat.

## Chapter 7 / *Behind the Numbers*

The firemen were battling to contain the furiously blazing fires and trying to prevent a spread to the other buildings on the property.

Two emergency medical units had pulled into the edge of the fire zone and attendants were hurrying about, checking life signs among the victims.

Uniformed officers cautiously poked about the grounds, while photographers and other police specialists preserved various items of hard evidence.

Captain Wayne Thomkins, Chief of Special Details for the Philadelphia Police Department, stood at the edge of the scene with a small group of state and federal officers. The Captain's face was a study in anger, bafflement—perhaps embarrassment. He asked the FBI representative on the Bolan task force what must have been a purely rhetorical question to all others present. "Well, what's the verdict? Was it a Bolan hit?"

Agent Joseph Persicone nodded his head and murmured, "I'd say so. It's fairly typical. He usually leaves a mess like this."

"I see it but I still can't believe it," the Captain said. "I don't see how one man, acting alone, can. . ."

"I don't either, but he does it," Persicone insisted.

"The medics have already tabulated fifteen dead.

God knows how high the count will go when we start through the rubble."

"That's typical too," the agent said, sighing.

Another plain-clothes officer stepped into the group and whispered something in Thomkins' ear. The Captain nodded and said, "I sure do. Send him over."

The cop hurried away.

Persicone asked, "What was that?"

"We had a stake-out here," Thomkins replied, the red of his face seeming to deepen. "We're getting the guy in here now to get his story."

One of the men in the group snickered and commented, "Some stake-out."

"We're on EPA here," the Captain growled. He was referring to the "Extreme Precaution Apprehension" routine. "Let's hear what the man has to say."

It was a high-echelon group attending this aftermath of a massive Executioner strike. Persicone was chief of a special federal strike force which had been turned onto the chase for Mack Bolan. Also present were too high-rankers from the state's criminal division, plus one of the top men of Philadelphia County. Others, many others, were busily setting up control-room operations downtown in an effort to contain Bolan's Philadelphia plans as much as possible. They had been racing the clock in an attempt to move ponderous machinery into place ahead of the approaching night. Obviously they had lost the race. Bolan was already loose and blitzing. In a city the size of Philadelphia, with all its normal problems, it was not easy to react quickly to a situation such as this one.

Thomkins' face seemed to be dwelling upon thoughts similar to this as the group of officials waited in restrained silence and watched the approuch of a young plain-clothes officer.

The newcomer seemed nervous, somewhat apprehensive, as he introduced himself as "Detective Strauss". He extended a small leather notebook to Captain Thomkins and told him, "That's the story, sir. Second by second, blow by blow."

The Captain grunted and riffled the pages of the notebook without looking at it. He went right to the point, asking, "Where were you, Strauss?"

The detective pointed toward the southeast corner of the property. "Right around the corner, on Parklane. I even saw the guy go over the wall, Cap'n. I can't be sure of this, I mean I'm not dead positive but—well, I believe the guy was around here all afternoon. I think I even talked to him. He came over and got a light from me, small-talked for a minute or two."

Thomkins shot a quick glance at the FBI agent. Persicone grimaced and nodded his head in an affirmative reply to the mute question.

"All right, tell us about that," the Captain said to Strauss.

The young officer was losing his nervousness. He fixed the Captain with a steady gaze and told him, "He was driving a phone company truck, or at least I took it for one. And he was outfitted like a lineman. Climbing poles and stringing wire all around here, all afternoon. About, uh, five o'clock he was working the pole just down from me. Came over and asked for a light. Said something about not carrying enough matches for overtime. Asked me how much longer I'd have to hang around the neighborhood. I asked him what he meant—I was just waiting for a friend. He laughed, said okay, I could stick with that story if I wanted to. Asked me if the big joint back there was still a whorehouse. I said how the hell would I know. He laughed again and went back to work. I didn't start to connect the guy until—"

"Just a minute," Thomkins interrupted. "You're saying the guy tumbled that you were a police officer on stake-out? Is that—?"

"Yessir, he knew. We get that all the time, you know. Everyone seems to delight in fingering the fuzz."

One of the officials commented, "You're on the Bolan detail, right? You were here specifically to spot any smell of the guy in this neighborhood, around this known mob hangout. I presume you've been briefed on Bolan's tricks, his M.O. You've seen the artists' sketches, I'm sure. And yet you. . . ?"

Strauss colored, but stuck his chin a bit higher in the reply. "I called in and asked for a phone company verification when I first noticed this lineman. I got a confirmation that work was scheduled for this area but that's all I could get. Somebody at headquarters was supposed to be checking it out but I never heard any more about it. Meanwhile, the guy was going about his business like he knew what he was doing. I had no reason to suspect that he—"

"All right, Strauss," Thomkins put in. "This isn't a civil service hearing. No one's accusing you of dereliction. What else do you have to tell us? You said you saw him going over the wall?"

"Yessir. I'm pretty sure it was him, I mean the same guy, the lineman. The place where he went over was a bad angle for me, though. I mean, it was just a flash glimpse, but I'm sure he came out of that phone company truck—and then, flash, he's going over the wall and out of sight. He'd *been* wearing this jumpsuit, you know, coveralls—like some linemen wear—the tool kit, spikes, all that. But he's hitting that wall now rigged up for *war*, I mean heavy combat. But it was a bad angle, and I guess I sat there for a couple of seconds wondering if I'd actually seen what I thought I'd seen. You know how those things go. You're sitting there for hours, looking for something—then when you *see* it, you wonder if your eyes are leaping at ghosts. Well . . . then I called in the contact report and dispatch ordered me to stay with the car. And I did, until the shooting started. I reported that also, then went out to see what I could see. All hell was breaking loose by then. I mean explosions, fire, the whole bit."

Thomkins was glaring at something in the detective's notebook. "You sure these times are right?" he asked in a muffled voice.

"Yessir. I paid particular attention to that. You can check it out with dispatch. Those are the exact times—"

58

"You're saying two minutes or less," Thompkins said in that same muffled tone. "You're saying the guy raised all this hell in just *two minutes?*"

"Ninety seconds, sir," Strauss reported, tight-lipped. "Exactly. He was ninety seconds inside those walls, that's all."

"That's all," the Captain echoed.

"Yessir. I was running along the road just outside the wall, trying to get in close enough to read the license on that panel truck. The guy came back over the wall before I could get halfway there; then all those smaller buildings went to hell. When the smoke cleared, the guy was gone. Some of those inside left at about that time also. I saw two big limousines streaking out the back way."

Persicone muttered, "And the Don got away."

"Sir?"

Thomkins was working at another angle of thought. He snapped, "Then how did we . . . ?" He stabbed a finger at an aide and barked, "Time of response!"

"Five forty-two," the man replied, without referring to notes. "Fire department also responded at that same time. Citizen's report, gunshots and fire at the corner of—"

The Captain's eyes were all but rolling in their sockets as he cut into the report with a snarl at Persicone: "Four minutes *before* Strauss called in *his* contact, before the show even started. So who the hell called, Joe? Don't tell me . . . *don't.*"

The FBI man was studying his watch. With a half-smile playing at his mouth, he murmured,

"What'd it take us to get out here? . . . About five minutes?"

"About that!" Thomkins snapped.

"Probably called it in from a pole," Persicone decided, openly grinning now. "I'd say he timed it pretty close—closer than I'd care to try. He calls the cops and the firemen, romps in, knocks the joint over, slides out—and he's got half of official Philadelphia protecting his withdrawal. Pretty cute, eh?"

"Hell, I can't buy that," the Captain growled.

"You will," the FBI man assured him. "Right now, I believe we'd better start worrying about his next punch. It will be coming, and soon. We'd better start figuring where."

"No worry there," Thomkins snarled. "All we have to do is sit back and wait for his next call!"

The FBI agent shifted his gaze to the young detective, Strauss. He showed him a sympathetic smile and asked him, "Could you give us an accurate reading of that lineman's face? Could you describe it in pretty fair detail to a police artist?"

The embarrassed officer dropped his eyes from that knowing gaze and replied, "I guess not, sir. To tell the truth, I never got a really clear look at that face, sir."

Persicone nodded understandingly and told Captain Thomkins, "You can see the size of our problem, Wayne. We're not simply going against another wanted man, or some kind of nut. We're up against a genius, a real pro, a guy who knows every trick in the combat book, an infiltration specialist, a method actor and—"

"And a blitz artist," Thomkins interrupted, sighing. "A brazen bastard, at that. He knew we had the place under surveillance. He drops in on our cop and lets him *know* he knows. Then he just waltzes over and. . . Okay. Okay, Joe. I'm buying the guy. Where do I make my down payment?"

"Let's go ask Don Stefano about that," Persicone suggested. He smiled, a droll flick of lips and eyes, and added, "If there's still time."

Bolan was pushing his luck with the warwagon and he knew it. The time had come to dump it and switch to something less noticeable. However, he had followed the Don's vehicles from the Emperor's to a sedate neighborhood on the near north side of town and satisfied himself that the old man was indeed going home—and he had one final job to perform with this disguised war machine.

There had never been any thought of mounting a frontal assault upon the Angeletti residence. There was no combat stretch in that neighborhood. Houses were too close together, too near the street where too much traffic flowed; the odds were simply too great that innocent civilians would get caught in the action.

That house did figure in certain other aspects of the war, though—and the time would never be better to take this initiative.

Bolan felt that he had to chance it.

He had engineered a tap on Angeletti's telephone two days earlier and left the splice taped off at a distribution box located a block and a half away from the house. Using his lineman's phone, he could connect into that circuit whenever the time seemed appropriate to do so.

That time had now arrived.

He made one pass through the neighborhood in the wake of Angeletti's limousines, verified their destination, then circled about in a quick recon of the area.

And, yeah.

The cops had this place under surveillance, also.

He spotted two likely, appropriately inconspicuous cars angled off for unobstructed views of the front of the Angeletti home, another on a side street where the rear of the property could be watched via a narrow alleyway.

They were not watching for Angeletti.

They were waiting for Mack Bolan.

It was a police tactic which was giving Bolan more trouble than all the others. Not that he blamed the cops. It was their job. They weren't trying to protect the enemy, necessarily—although in the curious legal-moral structure of this country the lawless had as much right to protection under the law as anyone else. But that wasn't it. The cops were probably just as happy as anyone to see these Mafia fatcats—whom they could rarely touch, themselves—falling all over their asses trying to evade the Executioner's implacable style of justice. But supposedly it was a nation of law. And the law had to prevail. Mack Bolan had to be put out of circulation.

And the law was gunning for Mack Bolan in Philadelphia.

Sure, he accepted that. It was part of the game. Bolan had never asked for a hunting license; he'd even refused one, early in the game.

But the cops were *not* the enemy. They were, in Bolan's mind at least, soldiers of the same side. He could not fight them. He could only hope to avoid them. And they were making that task more and more difficult all the time.

He warily circled the neighborhood, counting his chances and calculating probabilities. Then he threw the whole thing into the hands of the universe and sent the warwagon along the side street to the north of the Angeletti address.

It was a short block and a narrow street—no houses fronting, no streetlamps. Night had fallen. The moon was up, but high trees on the properties bordering to each side were casting deep shadows and enveloping the narrow lane in heavy darkness.

He could not have asked for better conditions.

With the exception of the AutoMag and the Beretta, he left his armaments in the warwagon and went up the pole to eavesdrop on a *Capo*.

The line was in use when he plugged in.

Someone in the household was talking to a doctor, one who presumably knew how to keep his mouth shut about certain injuries which could prove embarrassing to a low-profile family like the Angeletti *Mafiosi*.

A few seconds after the conclusion of that conversation, old man Angeletti himself made a call to an attorney. This had to do with certain protective measures which the Don had apparently worked out some time earlier, something to do with a dummy lease which had been let on the Emperor's property, and "you know what to say when the cops come nosing around."

The lawyer assured the *Capo* that he could not possibly be tied, not officially anyway, to the trouble out at the Emperor's.

The third call was made immediately thereafter —a direct-dial long distance connection into a New York City exchange—and Bolan knew that this one was the paydirt he'd been awaiting.

A cautious voice responded to the third ring with a quiet, "H'lo, yeah, who's that?"

Don Stefano's voice announced, "This is me in Philly."

"Oh, yeah, we just been talking about you." Bolan recognized this voice as belonging to one Augie Marinello, boss of all the bosses everywhere. "Listen, be careful. They found our, you know, stuntbox. So we're talking plain out."

"Yeah, I know," Angeletti replied. "How much longer before we, uh, get another one? I really need to talk to you."

Bolan understood the meaning of "stuntbox". It was a rig similar to a scrambler which automatically encoded/decoded telephone conversations—a security measure against phone taps.

"Another day or two," Marinello was saying. "Maybe you better just come in."

"I can't. Listen. It's really bad here."

A brief silence, then: "That's what we been talking about."

"Is everybody there? I mean, all of you?"

"Yeh," said the unofficial *Capo di tutti Capi*. "We been having a session, wondering what we could do for you."

"Well, listen. You can do a lot. I want everybody that's ever seen this guy before, I mean the merest glimpse. How'm I supposed to spot a guy that nobody's ever seen before, huh? Listen, you got somebody that's even smelt his farts, I want that some-body here with me. This thing is getting bad."

"'There's not many of that kind around," Marinello replied quietly.

"There's a few," the old Don argued. "There's that Leo the Pussy. You sent him all the way to London. Why not send him to Philly for a short vacation? I could use the guy. And, uh, that nigger. From Washington. You know? Our late friend Arnie's controller. What's his name, the football guy?"

"Wils Brown," Marinello said, sighing.

"That's the guy. I need 'im here."

"He's not one of us."

"Who cares? Let's not be proud. At a time like this. Right?"

"Right, I guess so," the third voice from New York agreed. "Listen, Steven—I don't wanta say too much. But . . . we been putting heads together here. We're sending you, uh, some help. So relax. Uh . . . maybe you better tell me. What's going on there now?"

"That guy just now walloped the hell out of us. *You* tell *me* how, I don't know, I really don't. I never saw nothing like this. Hey, the Bronx was never like this, not even back when."

"Anybody I know get carried out of the game?" Marinello asked.

"Not all the way. Our friend Jules is going to have some pain for a while, but he's okay. The rest was those, you know, those boys from over there. I think maybe twenty or thirty won't be with us no more."

"Gee, *that many,* that's too bad," Marinello said, the tone shocked and sympathetic.

"I still got plenty more, but I don't know. I mean, you know, those boys didn't stop a thing. I mean, like paper dolls. I'm not so sure about these boys, Augie."

"Yeah." A pause, then, "I guess we can talk about that later. Right now, I want you to feel assured. You know. We're not letting you down. We got a . . . listen . . . I can't say too much . . . we got a specialist on the way to you. He's—just a minute."

Bolan heard off-telephone whispers, then Marinello's voice came back directly into the line. "He's on his way there now. Driving. Look for him in about another thirty minutes."

"One guy?" old man Angeletti fumed. "Just one guy?"

"Well, one, yeah, but not *just* a guy, Steven. I told you, a specialist. Listen . . . relax. This guy is recommended by the very best. Our friend Mike sends his best."

Bolan also remembered their friend Mike. Talifero. Bolan had last seen their friend Mike lying in his own blood on a Vegas casino floor.

"I thought Mike was . . . is he up and around now?" Angeletti was asking, voicing Bolan's own interest in the matter.

"He's getting around some now. He's here now, right beside me. Sends you his best, Steven. You understand me."

"I understand you," the old man replied, sighing. "But one man, Augie. . ."

"Oh, we're sending more than just the one. Buffalo is sending down a delegation. We got a couple groups leaving Manhattan in another hour or two. You know, it takes awhile to round these delegations up. And with, uh, you know, our little troubles over in Brooklyn, uh. . ."

"Yeah, I know," the Philly boss said, understanding. "Well, I appreciate everything you can do, Augie. You know that. This thing is looking real serious. This, uh, specialist. Do I know him?"

A pause, then, "Mike says you do and you don't. Nobody really knows this guy, Steven."

"Oh, *that* guy!" Angeletti crowed, the old voice crackling with new interest.

"Yeh. So, look, take it easy, eh? Just keep yourself covered the best you can and let nature take its course. Everything is in our favor, you know that."

"Sure, okay, you know how much I appreciate—listen, I still want those other guys I mentioned. Leo the Pussy and the football player. And any more you might know about."

"That might be hard to engineer, Steven. But I'll try. You have my word."

"Look, it's no time to be holding out trumps," Angeletti pointed out.

"I know that. We're not holding anything out on you, Steven. You have my word. How's, uh, how's Frank?"

"Frank's just fine," Frank's papa reported. "I been real proud of him today."

It was a lie. Bolan knew it, and he knew that Marinello knew it.

"It's nice to have a son who can take some of the

pressures away," Marinello was saying. "Most of 'em today aren't worth a damn. You know that, Steven."

"Yeah, I know that," Angeletti agreed stiffly.

"Well, I know it's a comfort to have a good strong son in the house. I never had a one with legs under 'im. You know that. But . . . we gotta accept some things. Right? We gotta learn to live with pain sometimes."

It was a gentle hint from the boss of bosses to the boss of Philly. Bolan knew it. Angeletti knew it. The old man sighed and told New York, "Frank's coming along. Don't worry, Augie, I'm no idiot. I know what I know. Well, listen. I better hang up. I got a jillion things to do. That, uh, that specialist. How will I know him?"

A whispered consultation preceded: "Mike says you'll know him when he wants you to."

"I need more than that," Angeletti complained. "We're not taking chances on anything that moves around here. You better give me something for recognition."

A new voice came on from the New York end, a hard businesslike talker with a Harvard accent that set Bolan's teeth on edge. It was Mike Talifero, lord high enforcer of all *mafiosi* everywhere. "Steven, hello, I've been listening in. Do you understand who it is we're sending you?"

"Hi, Mike, sure I know who you're sending. Problem is, the guy's a wild card. Never the same face two times outta the deck. I gotta know what to look for."

"Look for a Maserati."

"A *what?*"

"You know, a car. That's what he's driving. Just let him in the gate. He can handle the ID from there."

"Oh, I get you. I guess that's good enough. You just better hope the guy doesn't switch cars on the way."

Talifero laughed and replied, "No way. He just blew his last dollar on that bucket. Listen, Steven. This boy is good. Give him his head. Don't try to tie him down."

"You sending him down here to take charge?" Angeletti asked soberly.

"It's the only way he works, Steven. You know that."

"Yeah. Well. I been letting Frank run herd on . . . on these boys here."

"Let's be men, Steven."

"I see what you mean. Okay." The old man sighed heavily and said, "Put Augie back on."

Marinello reported, "I'm still here, Steven. Listen. Soon as this all blows over, come up and see us. We need to have a long talk."

"Yeh. Thanks, Augie. And thank all our friends up there for me. Oh, and don't forget, you're sending me more than just this wild card from Mike."

"I'll do all I can, Steven."

"Thanks. 'bye, Augie."

"Good-bye, Steven."

Bolan waited until both clicks canceled the connection entirely, then he pulled his patch out and pushed that conversation through his mind several times around.

Things could be coming to a head quicker than he'd expected. Bolan had heard about this "wild card"—a Talifero trouble-shooter who carried *Commissione* credentials and who acted with all the authority of that ruling Mafia body.

The guy was an elite hit-man. He was usually saved for very special jobs, like hitting outside VIP's who'd earned themselves a contract, or errant *capi* who refused to knuckle under to *Cosa Nostra* edicts. The rumors were out that this very same "wild card" had been very busy of late in Brooklyn and Jersey.

Bolan had once impersonated the guy.

Maybe, just maybe, the Philadelphia problem was deserving of an encore performance by Mack the Wild Card Bolan.

But . . . the wild card could turn out to be a Black Jack. Few men living had ever seen Mack Bolan's face clearly enough to recognize it the next time around.

Leo Turrin could, of course.

So could Wilson Brown.

It could get sticky, damned sticky. One slip, one wrong jerk of the eyes or catch in the voice and. . .

Hell, he could *try*, couldn't he?

Maybe not.

Maybe he'd never try anything, ever again.

A police cruiser wheeled into the intersection just above Bolan's position and halted there, sealing the narrow street. Another had eased up just down-range from him, at the opposite corner. And suddenly the Executioner sensed movements on the ground all about him.

A spotlight flared, pinning him to the pole in the brilliance, and an electronically amplified voice wafted up from the darkness somewhere out there:

*"Mack Bolan, this is the law. You're sealed in. Throw down your weapons, one by one."*

So okay.

He'd pushed the thing one damn number too far.

*"Don't crowd us, Bolan. We're going to take you, dead or alive. It's your choice. Five seconds, man. Don't crowd us."*

Bolan was not crowding anybody.

He was simply hanging there, in the spotlight, seeing the end of a very vicious, very tiring and very brutal war.

It looked as though the hands of the universe had decided to rid themselves of Mack the Bastard.

## Chapter 9/ *An Intervention*

Capture by the police could have but one meaning for Bolan.

He would be stripped defenseless and placed inside a box where his million and one enemies could take turns trying to potshot him out of there.

Sure, the law would give him all the protection at their command. He would be treated like a VIP and accorded the most stringent security that probably any prisoner would ever find. Bolan, after all, was quite an authority on the mob, its operations, its chain of command, its inroads into various legitimate business areas. A dozen crime committees and federal agencies would love to get into his mind.

Also, he had become something of a folk hero. Some of the most prominent trial lawyers in the country had publicly proclaimed that they would like to represent the Executioner if and when he should fall into police hands.

Somebody would probably want him to write a book from Death Row, and probably every magazine in the country—and maybe a few movie producers—would be fighting for exclusive exploitation rights to his personal "story".

Sure, it would be quite a circus.

Except for one flaming fact.

None of it would ever have time to come to pass. Despite the security, the lawyers, the hoopla and the sensational public interest angle—despite it all —Bolan would not live through the first twenty-four hours in jail. Someone, somehow, would get to him. The mob had their ways. They would find a way to him. *We're going to take you dead or alive. It's your choice.* What choice? There was no choice for Mack Bolan. Except to die like a rat in a trap . . . or to die trying. He had elected, long ago, to die trying.

The little Doomsday Device was clipped to his utility belt, an inch and a half away from the hand that held him to the telephone pole.

He closed that gap between life and death, quickly and decisively, letting go and pushing off with his feet to arc over backwards in free-fall towards the ground, out of the hateful glare of that police spotlight—and in that same instant he found the doomsday button and triggered the charge in the warwagon.

A shotgun had *ba-loomed* out there the moment he moved, and other weapons immediately chimed in for the kill, but all—the night, the cacophony of gunfire, the death-reel in Bolan's brain—all of it was eclipsed and set aside by the earth-shaking blast of the warwagon as it went into self-destruct and lent its parts to the expanding universe.

Bolan had been going for a catlike backflip away from the pole, trusting entirely to instinct to bring him to earth in the most survivable position, feet down, crouched for impact absorption, his senses flaring out into the darkness for some split-second orientation and warning before the shock of contact came.

The shock of the explosion came first, however, and some frozen timeless compartment of the Bolan mind knew that he was too close and that he was being deflected in mid-air, hurled sideways by the concussive force of that blast—being hurled, perhaps, into infinite timelessness.

Then he was into something soft-solid, something that moved with him and cushioned, something that seemed to reach out and gather him in. His spinning mind seized around the idea of the hands of the universe reaching out to snatch him back even while some tenaciously clinging fragment of consciousness told him that the cushioning bosom belonged instead to a sweet-smelling tree in Spring blossom.

Outflung arms instinctively closed around softly supporting young branches, and he swung on like some weirdly costumed ape, without seeing and without really *knowing,* moving swiftly from limb to limb and then down free and clear onto the ground.

He crouched there in well-cultivated shrubbery, willing his mind and his systems to stabilize, fighting an advancing curtain of inner darkness, which could only be unconsciousness or perhaps death.

That compartment of mind which *knew* seized upon the abundant stimulations of the immediate environment to drag him through crisis and into reality, tugged him into a recognition of leaping flames, excited voices and bawling commands issuing from an electronic amplifier.

And he knew with a jolt that he was alive and—by some miracle—functioning, separated from the threat out there by a low brick wall, screening shrubbery, and monumental confusion.

He wished the cops well, genuinely hoped that none of those soldiers on the same side had been close enough to run afoul of the warwagon's final contribution to Mack Bolan's war effort—and he left them there with his well-wishes and moved quietly out with the shadows into the no man's land of Don Stefano's home grounds.

Bolan was not afraid, but as cool as life resurrected.

He was "retreating to the front"—bolstered, strengthened and revitalized by the certain knowledge that something far larger than himself had worked some sort of miracle.

The universe had intervened. The Executioner was alive and kicking in Philadelphia.

For the moment, anyway.

## Chapter 10/ *The Benediction*

The firefighters had come, found no remaining fires to extinguish, and departed—leaving only a cleanup crew and an arson/bomb squad at the scene.

Fifty wary and heavily armed cops were scouring every inch of ground in the immediate vicinity.

Just for kickers, a special squad was awaiting arrival of a search warrant to get them into the Angeletti property to extend the search into that unlikely area.

An emergency medical crew was on hand, smoking and drinking coffee from paper cups and wondering why they were there.

A police bomb squad, lab men and every dicky kind of specialist the department could dream up had arrived; and began fine-combing the street, the wreckage and a fifty-yard radius around the blast area.

The scene was sealed off completely and additional roadblocks were set up to contain a four-square-block area of the surrounding neighborhood.

Emergency telephone and power company crews had been summoned, but orders had been left at the blockade to keep them out until further notice.

Sullen clumps of uniformed and plain-clothes policemen had returned to the ground-zero area to stand around looking helpless during these anticlimactic moments.

A disconsolate Chief of Special Details, Captain Wayne Thomkins, had been standing with hands in pockets for some five minutes, staring steadfastly at the ground between his feet.

FBI Agent Joe Persicone was kneeling a respectful distance from the twisted pile of hot metal which marked the remains of Mack Bolan's last known vehicle, staring at it as though he could unlock its secrets through some process of psychic osmosis.

Detective Ed Strauss, who had been added to the main body of Bolan Watchers upon their departure from the Emperor's hit, vaulted over the low brick wall which bounded the private property on the south side of the street and strode up to break into Captain Thomkins' meditations.

Thomkins glowered at the young officer and growled, "Yeah?"

The detective spread his hands at shoulder level and replied, "Zero, nothing."

The Captain sighed and said, "Can't catch moonbeams in a fruit jar, can you?"

"Sir?"

"Forget it." Thomkins paced over to the wall and glared at it. "Should've found him right here," he said. "His back broke over this wall."

Strauss was measuring the distance with his eyes, mentally triangulating the drop from a point in space where the pole had been, probably re-enacting in his mind's eye that spectacular free-fall into nowhere. His gaze traveled that imaginary path and he shuddered as it rebounded from the brick wall. "Yessir," he quietly agreed. "That was my first impression. I saw the guy go sailing off that pole backwards and I remember thinking, 'Far out, what a way to go!' I fully expected to—"

"So what's your second impression?" Thomkins asked somberly.

"Sir?"

"Where'd he go?"

Strauss raised his hands in what was becoming a characteristic gesture as he replied, "Hell, I can't imagine. I've been thinking about those trees over there, just inside the wall. It's not inconceivable that . . ."

"Glad you said that," Thomkins growled in a somewhat softened tone. "Saved me from saying it. What'd he do, whip out his Batman cape and *fly* over there?"

"A superb athlete could . . . well, maybe. I don't know, Cap'n. I just said it's not inconceivable."

Persicone stood up with a sigh and joined the debate.

"It's a purely academic question," he suggested. "We have to accept the obvious. Bolan fell right into the blast and was annihilated."

"You know better than that," Thomkins replied acidly. "That's a cop-out and you know it. You were right at my elbow. You saw the whole thing as clearly as I did. And you saw the guy falling away in the *other* direction, *away* from the blast."

The FBI man lit a cigarette and blew the smoke toward the gutted truck. "Eyes can play tricks," he said. "Especially at a time like that. All we saw was the guy falling out of the spot. We were all so tensed up we were ready to jump at anything. We *projected* a path of fall, away from the spot, which was the only light available at the moment. But away *where?* Away *down,* that's where; it was the only route the guy had. Then the blast came, and suddenly we had a lot more light than our eyes could handle. Face it, we lost the guy the instant he left that pole. By the time our eyes adjusted to all that light—and our minds, I might add, to the whole unsettling event—well, all I'm saying is that we *thought* him into that path-of-fall. We don't know what the hell we saw."

"I know what *I* saw," Thomkins insisted.

"Look, Wayne, look—we were a half a block away. You've got to consider the darkness, the angle of vision, the sudden blindness from the blast. Let's let logic make the decision. We did not find a broken body, not even any blood. We covered every inch of the surrounding area, we searched the trees, we've looked into every conceivable fall-zone. Now, I don't care how superb the athlete or anything else—no guy is going to get up from a fall like that and simply walk away, or even crawl away. So . . . we are left with one inescapable conclusion."

"I'll buy that conclusion," Thomkins growled, "when I can find something factual to pin it to."

Persicone smiled faintly and said, "You're a stubborn cop."

"Thank you," Thomkins replied.

Strauss said, "With your permission, Cap'n . . . I'd like to have the firemen assist me with—I'd like them to lift me in that bucket of their's."

80

"Yeah, go ahead," the head cop agreed. "Just don't try any swan dives outta that bucket."

Strauss grinned and hurried away.

The two men watched his departure for a moment. Then Persicone quietly declared, "That's a good man."

"Yeah," Thomkins agreed. "He doesn't buy your theory either, Joe."

"He's got a personal interest in this case now," the FBI man pointed out. "Bolan left him with egg all over his face."

"Not just *him*," Thomkins observed sourly.

An embarrassed silence enveloped the pair. Thomkins returned to his eyes-on-toes meditation. Persicone began pacing back and forth between the shattered telephone pole and the brick wall.

Presently a fire captain ambled up, grinning. He snapped a curious glance at the pacing FBI agent, then told Thomkins, "It's subject to lab verification but I think I can tell you what triggered the explosives. My boys are putting some pieces together. Looks like a remote-control detonator."

"Radio?"

"Yeah. Solid-state miniature."

The cop said, "Okay, that fits our theory. Put some more pieces together, will you, Cap? Find me some toes and fingers, even an eyeball or a testicle. Find me a piece of the guy that pushed the plunger."

"If he was in that truck," the fireman replied, "you can probably forget it. It's a miracle nobody else got hurt. It appears that the blast went *up* more so than *out,* which accounts for the small-area containment. Your bomb boys agree with us on that. It's possible to plan an explosion that way; maybe the guy did. Anyway, if he went *up* with it—well, forget the pieces."

The fire captain threw another glance at Persicone and walked away.

The FBI man stopped his pacing and told the cop in charge of the Bolan detail, "I'm not telling you your business, Wayne."

"Okay, don't."

"Yeah, stubborn, yeah."

Another silence ensued, during which the two of them interestedly watched a young detective who was being swung high overhead in a fire department emergency rescue rig.

While this was in progress, the two-way radio on Thompkins' belt summoned him, and delivered the information that the search warrant was awaiting him near the Angeletti front gate.

"Okay, hold it right there," he instructed the caller. "I'll be over there in a couple of minutes."

"Waste of time," Persicone commented, with a faint smile.

"We'll see," Thomkins told him. "Want to come along?"

"Even if the guy *did* walk away, would he take refuge at Don Stefano's joint?"

"You're the Bolan expert," the cop replied. "Would he?"

Persicone sighed and said, "Hell, he might."

A loud whoop sounded from overhead, halting the two men in their tracks as they trudged toward their vehicle.

The bucket rig was swung out over the adjoining grounds and nestling into one of the trees which lined the wall over there. Strauss, his face glowing in the beam from the rig's spotlight, was waving something in his hand and shouting down at them.

"It's a *pocket,* Cap'n!" he yelled. "A *black* pocket off a uniform! *Ripped* off, not burned!"

"There you go," Thomkins declared in a half-audible reaction to the find.

"Give that boy a promotion and a cigar," Persicone commented.

"Bullshit," said the chief of the get-Bolan detail. "It would've been easier the other way. That ties it, you know. That just flat out ties it."

They were hurrying to the car now.

Persicone said, "There's no sweetness to the victory, eh?"

"Victory, what victory?" the Captain retorted. "If we don't find the guy at Angeletti's, do you know what I'm going to do next?"

The FBI man was grinning. "I'll bite. What?"

"I'm going to assign a fire truck and an ambulance to the guy. And then I'm going to go home, get drunk, and go to bed."

Persicone chuckled and said, "You're glad he made it and you know it."

"Get screwed," the Bolan-chaser growled.

The tart rejoinder could have been a benediction.

For sure, the confusion over Mack Bolan's free-fall fate had added the edge to make it a night for miracles.

## Chapter 11/ *Contained*

Bolan had scouted the area thoroughly two days earlier, even drawing sketches of the grounds with topographical notes of terrain irregularities and plotting probable floor layout of the house interiors.

It was one of several similar two-story residences on that block, in a neighborhood which was classed as "upper-middle".

It was about a one-acre plot, and the house took up much of that.

There was a brick wall on all four sides, a fancy iron gate with remote-control locks operable from a vehicle or from the house, a winding drive that skirted the property and took all the advantage there was of the limited ground area, circling to the back and through the carport, then back down to the gate. Made it look like a great deal more than it was.

The *Capo*'s next-door neighbor was a pediatrician. The man across the street was regional sales rep for a paint company. Another neighbor was a retired university professor.

It was an affluent neighborhood, but not a "rich" one.

Bolan had learned that Angeletti had lived here for twenty-two years, since just after the death by pneumonia of his wife. It seemed to be all the home that the widower needed or wanted, with both the kids off to school during the earlier years and flinging around with their own things after that.

There were no grandchildren—not even a son-in-law or daughter-in-law.

Philippa had been ten when her mother died.

Maybe that was why, said idle tongues, she had never learned to act like a woman.

Bolan had heard no explanations for why Frank had never learned to act like a man. In some ways, sure, Frank the Kid managed. It was said that he'd laid every hooker in Philadelphia and adjacent areas. Only hookers, though—Frank had never shown a serious interest in any woman.

So, sure, it was a good enough "home" for Stefano Angeletti. He didn't have to impress anybody. Not lately. And there were no embarrassing questions from the federal tax people about how he could afford to live so high. Don Stefano did not live high, not in any way that showed.

There were ways that did not show, of course. Bolan had heard also of the "much fancier joints" tucked away here and there for those secret week ends and seasonal vacations. Retreats, they were called. But the stories had it that the only thing Angeletti ever retreated from was his own family.

He maintained a home for them—in which he stayed with them for tolerable periods—a home which was not really a home by any usual standard.

It was actually a business headquarters, around which was fabricated a synthetic and baldly hypocritical environment of togetherness and familial devotion, intermixed with gun-toting bodyguards, late-night comings and goings and "business deals", an occasional party of chosen ones, a steady procession of Philippa's lovers and Frank's hookers, and the ever-present tensions of a Mafia *Capo*'s struggle to maintain authority in a crumbling empire.

The Angeletti family had been in trouble for some time.

Some of that was attributable to Stefano's advanced years. He was seventy-four. He had ulcers, high blood pressure, hardening of the arteries, and failing kidneys. But he had a strong old heart and he was still as mean as sin.

Most of the problems had come from outside. Stefano had lost the protection of anonymity some years back, thanks to Kefauver, and later Bobby Kennedy and that sharp old bird from Arkansas, Senator McClellan. He'd been getting considerable harassment from the feds and, lately, from local police agencies as well.

Also, Stefano had been subjected to gentle but insistent pressures from *La Commissione* to refine and update his operations, to bring in some new blood, to beef up, consolidate and firm up the ties with the national organization.

Philly had been a family operation for much too long—it was an anachronism in the modern Mafia.

Augie Marinello had once tried to engineer a marriage between Philippa and a young turk from one of the New York families . . . purely as a business arrangement and to give the Don an alternate heir who could be regarded as "in the family".

But Philippa herself put the death seal on that idea, and the Don himself had not pushed the thing

86

since he'd not been overly enthusiastic over the project either.

Frank was the Angeletti heir, and *by God* Frank was going to get some legs under him some day even if Don Stefano had to manufacture some for him.

The *gradigghia* had apparently been intended to serve as Frank the Kid's artificial legs.

It took more than legs to make a *Capo*, however. It took a head, also, and nobody yet had figured out how to transplant a man's head onto a kid's shoulders.

Such was the status and the state of the Angeletti household on that night of unlikely nights when Mack Bolan came to call.

He had no clear idea of what he was going to do there, nor how. The Executioner was simply playing the game by ear, hoping to brazen his way out of an impossible situation and perhaps somehow to regain the initiative in a hopeless and decidedly unpopular war.

He was strongly aware of the fantastic odds which were quickly marshaling to the other side's favor.

He knew that the entire neighborhood was crawling with cops, that blockades were undoubtedly being set up to firmly contain him within a closely defined geographical trap—that it was only a question of time until once again he would be hearing that dreaded command, *"This is the law . . . throw down your weapons . . . dead or alive . . . your choice."*

But no . . . they wouldn't be saying it again. They would be shooting on sight, to kill—and actually he'd rather have it that way than the other. There was no decision to be made with a screaming bullet—no options, no alternatives.

It might even be a tossup as to whose bullets got to him first. This was no social club he'd ventured into. Angeletti had no less than twenty guns prowling this place, perhaps twice that since the Emperor's incident.

He had beefed-up gun crews coming down from Buffalo and Manhattan, plus an elite field general delegated by the boss of the storm troopers, Mike Talifero.

He had, maybe, also a couple of unsuspected wild cards in the personages of Leo Turrin and Wils Brown.

Wils had worked *with* Bolan on their last brush. But maybe that one had been simply for old time's sake, and maybe the war-maimed ex-football great had been kicking his butt ever since for not cashing in on that hundred-grand bounty collectible from Bolan's blood.

Leo Turrin was a great guy and a good friend. But he had his own thing to protect—and Bolan had always felt that a good cop would go on being a good cop above everything else. There was no way of ever being "for sure" about a cop—especially one who was himself balancing delicately above a chasm of certain disaster.

So . . . what else was there to play but the ear?

Three times in ten minutes Bolan had heard the tense breathings and cautious footfalls of the police bush-beaters right at the boundary of the Angeletti property.

Twice in as many minutes he had stood within touching range of curious Angeletti hardmen who were trying to figure out what was going on in the neighborhood.

Once the old man himself had appeared on a screened-in back porch to ask the yard chief, "Did'ja hear anything yet on that explosion?"

The reply had been to the effect that there had been a "car wreck or something down the block", and Angeletti then volunteered the information that, "Must'a been bad; our damn phones are out."

Another yardman muttered something about hearing gunshots mixed in with that explosion. Before Angeletti could comment on that, yet another man had come hoofing around from the front to announce, "Cops wanta come in to shake us down. They say this Bolan's in the neighborhood."

"Tell them to shake the neighborhood down, then," the old man barked. "We'll take care of our own!"

"They mean business," the hardman reported. "They say they'll get a warrant if they have to."

"Let 'em get their warrants then," Angeletti had replied, and slammed back inside the house.

So . . . sure . . . what else to play but the ear? What did a dead man have to lose?

And this was precisely the state of mind of the desperate warrior in black when the vehicle gate swung open and a gleaming foreign car—obviously of great value—eased onto the property, piloted, no doubt, by an elite "wild card" who had the whole wide bloody world to lose.

Chapter 12 / *Aces Wild*

Maserati it may have been, but it looked like a cruising shark as it crept silently along that winding drive. The top was down. The guy behind the wheel must have once been touched by the Grand Prix madness, or at least by the American image of how a European racing gentleman should look—or maybe it was the Red Baron Bolan was thinking of.

He was bareheaded, except for a white silk scarf draped vertically from the top of the head down, then swished across the throat and trailing out to the rear. He wore racing goggles and a white car-coat with the collar turned up.

Both car and man could have just driven out of an ad as an answer to "What sort of man reads *Playboy?*" This guy could have started the whole idea.

Most of what Bolan could see was an impression of a strong chin and plenty of good teeth as the Maserati came to a gentle halt at the intersection with the front walk.

The yard chief was standing there, a hand raised in the air in a silent command. He stepped forward to the driver's side and Bolan could hear the respectful challenge, "Identification please, sir."

The goggles went up and a strong, nicely modulated voice came back with, "How many times do I have to do this?"

"Sorry, sir. Routine." The yard boss accepted a

wallet-sized folder, looked at something inside there, and handed it back. "Glad you're here, Mr. Cavaretta," he said. "You can go in from here. I'll park the car for you."

The guy chuckled and replied, "The hell you will. I paid for it, I drive it, and I sure as hell park it."

"It's a beauty," the hardman said, backing off for a better look. "Must've cost some bucks."

"Try thirty thou' as a base, then work up through another ten in specials," said the playboy of the western underworld. After all, what comfort was a hunk of machinery like that if you couldn't flaunt it at somebody? Then he volunteered the information, "Just got her today. This is here maiden voyage."

"What'll she do? About one-fifty?"

"Try one seventy-five. I would have been here twenty minutes ago but—what gives with all the roadblocks around here? Thought I was crossing over the iron curtain or something."

"Aw, that guy, you know, our wise guy has been playin' games with us around here. Got all the cops in the state, I think, spooked up and chasin' shadows everywhere. They say he's in this neighborhood right now."

The guy in the forty-thousand-dollar shark laughed and said, "Let's hope so, eh? A hot blonde in New York is waiting for me to come home and cool her down."

The yardman laughed with him. "Think this will be a pretty quick one, huh, Mr. Cavaretta?"

"Quicker than you can learn to call me Johnny,"

91

the guy replied, and sent the car inching forward.

The wild card from New York had no idea how quick it was going to be.

A living shadow in combat black was pacing him across hell's last acre.

He pulled the gleaming vehicle into the end stall, stepped out, walked all the way around it once in an admiring inspection, then went to the front and raised the hood over the engine.

Bolan had moved into the shadows of the interior and was standing less than ten feet from the guy.

The yard chief was striding across the grounds, headed toward the gate out front.

Another yardman stood beneath the eaves of the house, about thirty feet from the carports. Still another was prowling slowly along the north wall, maybe fifty feet distant.

A fourth man came out of the house, carrying a cup of coffee; walked right past Bolan, and approached the Maserati. It was Frank Angeletti.

He stood at the front bumper of the car through a moment of awkward silence, then told the visitor, "Don Stefano knows you're here. He's waiting for you."

The guy didn't even look up. He said, "I'll be there in a minute. I think this damn thing is throwing oil."

"He's waiting," Frank the Kid repeated. He stood there in uncertain hesitation for a moment; then went back past Bolan's shadow and returned to the house.

Bolan felt a twinge of sympathy for the Kid. Must be hell, he was thinking, to try to fill a pair of shoes the size of Don Stefano's—especially when the old man insists upon walking around inside them all the time. What could a thoroughly domineering parent expect but a thoroughly dominated kid?

The Red Baron was still bent into the engine compartment, delicately feeling about with both hands and giving off disappointed grunts.

Bolan had taken Frank the Kid's place beside him.

He said, quietly, "Maybe you wound her up too high too soon."

The guy replied, "I'm going to wind her around someone's neck if what I think—I don't believe this gasket is. . ."

Bolan said, "Let me see," and reached in over the guy with both hands, behind him now, pressing against and leaning into his back, pinning him to the fender with his body.

The guy let out a muffled, "Hey, don't—"

The goggles squeezed up onto the curly hair and the silk scarf descended to shoulder level as Bolan's forearm found the soft flesh at the throat, to clamp off the dying protest.

The guy was strong.

The grimly silent struggle lasted perhaps five seconds before the fingers of Bolan's other hand twisted into the curly locks and the expertly applied "Vinh Ha torque" demonstrated its mastery over human anatomy. The victim's spinal column separated itself from the base of the skull with a grinding pop and the fight was over, the head lolling, body sagging into the ultimate relaxation.

Bolan let it drape itself across the fender while

he checked the positions of those outside; then he found the keys and opened the luggage compartment, stripped off his weapons and blacksuit and dropped them into there, undressed the guy and dropped *him* into there, and hastily pulled himself into the appropriated clothing.

The shirt fit okay but the trousers presented a small problem. The legs were too short, the waist too large. He fixed that by tugging the waist down into his hips.

The shoes were fancy ankle-high boots; he got into those all right, also, but at the expense of cramped toes.

The wallet was shiny new and so was everything in it. A driver's license identified one John J. Cavaretta, with a Manhattan address; as did private investigator's credentials issued by the State of New York, and a gun permit.

There were a dozen or more credit cards, a money clip containing five crackling fifties and a sheaf of twenties, plus a letter of credit from an Atlanta bank in the amount of fifty thousand dollars.

Half payment on Bolan's head? Maybe.

There was also a smaller leather case which folded into the wallet, displaying a single item in a swing-out transparent pocket. It was the size of a playing card. One side was made up like a business card, with a telephone number in the upper left corner plus a cable address. Gold-embossed letters at the center spelled in fancy Old English script the same name as on the other identification, *John J. Cavaretta.* Beneath the name were the words *Security Consultant.*

The other side *was* a playing card—the Ace of Spades.

This was the ID that counted—*Commissione* credentials.

Bolan pocketed the wallet and threw the car-coat into the seat to try on a double-breasted blazer Cavaretta had lying there. It fit fine and even featured an extra-wide cut on the left side to take care of the concealed weapon problem.

The guy had not been packing hardware, though.

Bolan found it in a small attache case behind the seat. Soft grain leather with a shoulder strap held a Browning standard automatic with a full thirteen-round clip, nine-millimeter, in the weapon plus a stack of spare clips—loaded. A special little pocket on the leather held a silencer.

So, good enough.

He closed the case and put it back, then rounded up the goggles and the scarf which had fallen to the ground during the struggle. He tucked the goggles in with the car-coat and draped the scarf about his neck.

Then he went back to the luggage compartment to study the "Security Consultant".

They didn't look much alike, except in generalities.

The guy had a strip of flesh-colored adhesive tape applied to each side of the lower jaw. Bolan pulled them off and found hair-width incisions, almost healed, running the full length of each jaw.

Cavaretta, or whatever his actual name, had recently undergone plastic surgery. The finding fit the legend of the guy.

It was said that he changed identities after each big job, getting a new face and everything that went with it.

A "wild card"—yeah.

Bolan transferred the adhesive strips to his own flesh and searched closely for other anomalies.

He found blue-tinted contact lenses riding the drying irises of the lifeless eyes, and left them there —he didn't need them.

Some sort of sort and transparent "living skin" adhesive covered each of the guy's finger tips.

Pretty cute, thought Bolan; it saved wearing conspicuous gloves and served the same purpose—no fingerprints left in awkward places.

He peeled off the finger patches and applied them to his own finger tips; tried them, found no appreciable loss of tactile perception.

Other perceptions, though, told him that he needed to hurry—movements out across the grounds and out beyond the grounds.

He was busy with the body when footsteps sounded near the front of the carport and someone called in to ask, "What's the trouble?"

It was time to try the voice. Bolan straightened up with an angry scowl and replied, "The trouble's going to be in New York when I get this bucket of bolts back there. I never saw such a disgraceful damn—"

"The old man's getting fidgety. Come on."

"Be right there," Bolan/Cavaretta assured the guy. "Give me a hand. Get that stuff off the seat and take it in. Oh, and pick up that case behind the seat, eh?"

Bolan had never set eyes on the guy before. He was probably one of the inside "boys". He came in and took the things from the car. Bolan was again "busy" in the luggage compartment.

"F' Christ sakes, sir, that old man is turning purple."

Bolan looked up with a grin. "Go hold his hand for a minute. I'll be right there."

The guy looked like he'd rather take a beating than return to the house without the guest in tow but he wheeled about and retreated, grumbling something beneath his breath as he trudged away.

Bolan was indeed very busy.

He was stuffing a dead, limp body into the black suit and rigging it for combat. He studied the final effect, adjusted the pants legs, then sighed and banged the trunk lid shut.

Those movements out across the grounds were becoming more pronounced, louder, and much more visible.

They were *beyond* the grounds and they were cops, droves of cops with flashlights forming an unbroken chain of manpower all along that wall over there.

The yard chief was rounding the corner of the house when Bolan stepped out of the carport. He gave Bolan a friendly wave and called over, "Maybe you got here just in time, Mr. Cavaretta. The cops are out front now with their fuckin' search warrant."

Bolan replied, "Good for them," and went on to the back door.

The guy with the gun-case and the car-coat was standing there in the open doorway waiting for him.

So, okay.

Mack the Wild Card Bolan/Cavaretta had just passed his first test. Another one awaited him just beyond that doorway.

And, yeah, that Ace of Spades had arrived just in the nick of time.

## Chapter 13/ *By the Ear*

He swept on past the guy and into the house, strode purposefully along the short rear hall, and hit the larger reception hall up front with coattails flying, his head swiveling rapidly from side to side in a fast absorption of the layout of the place.

Circular stairway going up from just inside the front door to a railed landing directly over the door—another short flight beyond that leading to an upstairs hallway and, presumably, the bedrooms.

Off to his left a large open doorway with velvet drapes, opening to a huge room with overstuffed heavy modern pieces, a lot of it, couches and chairs and tables everywhere. The largest color television receiver ever built was turned on but nobody was paying it much attention; ten or twelve men were in there, just sitting around, conversing in muted tones.

To Bolan's right was a set of massive folding doors, one side pushed back to the front wall—a large library-study-den-whatever visible through that opening. Four men were standing just inside that doorway. It was Frank the Kid, the *Caporegime* from South Philly—Carmine Drasco, a troubled-looking man of about fifty whom Bolan had never seen before, and the Don himself.

Bolan got in the first lick, asserting his authority. Addressing no one in particular and everybody collectively, he loudly declared, "The law is coming in. Let's get up on the toes, eh?"

He whipped off his blazer and snapped a commanding finger at the guy who'd trudged in behind him. "Open that case and give me what's in there, damn quick."

The guy fumbled the gun case open and tossed the rig over. Bolan caught it and slipped into it. Thank God the leather was adjusted perfectly for his frame.

As he secured the hardware he fixed Frank the Kid with a direct gaze and asked him, "How many of those boys outside are greasers?"

The Kid stumbled over the words a bit as he hastily replied, "What? No, they're not, none of them."

"So, where are they?"

"Laying low. We had a scatter plan. Don't worry, they're covered."

Bolan growled, "They damn well better be."

Old man Angeletti was giving the new arrival a hard stare—angry, yeah *angry*.

Bolan pulled on the blazer, left it unbuttoned, and muttered, "Thank something for small favors. Is everybody in here covered with paper?"

"What?" asked Frank the Kid.

Bolan grabbed the guy behind him, opened his coat, and relieved him of a snub-nosed nickle-plated revolver. He asked him, "Where's your paper for this?"

The guy's hand was shaking as he handed over the gun permit. Bolan glanced at it and threw it back at him. "It's *expired!*" he yelled. He jammed the pistol into the guy's holster and angrily commanded, "Ditch it! And you check every damn guy around here before those cops do!"

The hardman looked at Don Stefano and fidgeted.

Bolan yelled, *"Now!"*

Old man Angeletti put a hand on Frank's shoulder and gave him a little shove. "Help him," he ordered. "We don't want no embarrassing technicalities."

"You give 'em nothing, *nothing!*" Bolan yelled.

Frank and the hardman, who turned out to be the house captain, hurried into the large room across the hall.

Stefano was again giving Bolan the hard look. A serious breach of etiquette was being noted.

Bolan had done it deliberately. Now he went over to the Don, took his hand and kissed the withered skin. "Your friends in New York send their love and best wishes, Don Stefano," he announced in an appropriately respectful tone.

Angeletti nodded in mute acceptance of the courtesy. He was looking at the adhesive strips along Bolan's lower jaws. The thin old lips wobbled from side to side for a moment, then they parted and the Don asked the Executioner, "Did you get hurt or something?"

"I did and I didn't," Bolan replied, allowing a smile to come to his own lips.

Angeletti smiled back and said, "It's very pretty, very nice. Think they could do anything with a tired old face like this one?"

Bolan replied, "You might be surprised what

they can do today." It was time to "take over" again. He looked at Carmine Drasco and said, "Hi, Carmine. How're things Southside?"

The *Caporegime* showed him a somewhat embarrassed grin as he replied, "Great, great. Un . . . hell, I don't know what to call you."

The old man chuckled delightedly at that and crowed, "It's like *What's My Line*. Will the real what's-his-name please stand up?"

Bolan flipped the little leather folder away from the wallet and handed it over to Angeletti. The Don inspected it with great interest, then passed it on to Drasco.

The Southside lieutenant said, "Cavaretta, Caveretta . . . I used to know a . . . played guitar in a joint down on. . ."

Bolan heehawed and took the ID folder back.

Don Stefano was cackling something about a folk singer with an Ace of Spades in his pocket.

Then the front door cracked open and a guy poked his head inside to announce, "Okay, they're right outside."

"Get in here!" Bolan growled.

The guy slid in and banged the door shut.

Don Stefano, suddenly very flustered, had taken a little half-pirouette into the library.

Bolan told him gruffly, "Go on. I'll handle it."

The guy who'd brought the report went on into the crew room. Angeletti retreated into the library and went over to his desk.

Bolan was staring at the fourth man of that little committee-at-the-door, who had moved off just a little to one side. He said to Drasco, "I guess I don't know this gentleman."

Drasco said, "Oh, I'm sorry. Johnny, this is Doctor Kastler. He come to fix up—I guess you hadn't heard about—Doc, this is our very important friend from New York, Johnny Cavaretta."

Bolan acknowledged the awkward introduction with a quick flick of the eyes, ignoring the hand extended to him. He asked, "Who got hurt? Not gunshot, I hope."

The doctor said, "No, no, just a bit of first- and second-degree burns, arms and upper torso. He'll be all right."

Drasco explained, "Our friend Jules Sticatta. His clothes caught fire."

Bolan clucked his tongue and said, "I'm very sorry for our friend Jules."

The door chimes sounded.

Bolan commanded, "I'm handling this," and went to the door. His hand brushed something in the breast pocket of the blazer as he smoothed the jacket over his hardware, and he discovered in there a pair of gold wire-rimmed glasses with tinted lenses. He tried them, found a slight correction in the left lens but not enough to interfere with his own 20/20. Every little edge would help, at a time like this. He left them in place and swung the door open all the way, standing dead center and blocking entry with his own presence.

A passel of uniformed cops were on the front stoop, and others could be seen moving across the grounds.

A big sandy-haired guy in a gray suit and matching night-coat was standing just off the doorway, gazing out across the property. Another guy, a smaller Italian type, stood beside him giving Bolan the once-over.

Bolan said, "Did you come to look at the scenery or did you have some casual harassment in mind?"

The big cop turned to give him a frosty glare. He sighed and extended a folded, official-looking paper. "Here's my harassment chit," he growled.

Bolan did not even look at it. He said, "All right, come on in," and stepped out of the way.

The two plain-clothes men moved into the reception hall and the little posse of uniformed cops came in behind them.

Bolan commented, "So many to do so little?"

"Identify yourself, sir," the big cop snapped.

"You first," Bolan countered.

The cop flashed his badge.

Bolan grinned and said, "You have to do better than that."

"Who's harassing whom?" the guy growled, and held out the ID folder for Bolan's inspection. He looked at Drasco and nodded pleasantly. "Hello, Carmine," he said.

Drasco said, "Hi, Captain. You look tired."

"As hell," the cop said.

Bolan ignored that interplay, pushing the ID back and jerking his head toward the Italian. "Now him," he said.

That one wordlessly thrust FBI credentials under Bolan's nose.

Bolan said, "Is that a federal warrant you have there?"

The FBI guy said, "I have a right to be here but I'll wait outside if you'd rather."

"What's the difference, it's okay," Bolan replied, shrugging.

"Let's see your identification," the big cop reminded him.

"He's okay," Drasco put in. "I'll vouch for him."

The expression on the Captain's face seemed to say that he wouldn't let Drasco vouch for the mayor of Philadelphia.

Bolan tried to pass the wallet over but the cop, a Captain Thomkins, told him, "Hold it in your own hands, please, and just show me your driver's license."

Bolan said, "Suppose I don't drive?"

"You'd better have something to show me, mister."

Bolan grinned and displayed the New York driver's license, then the private eye ID. The cop's eyes showed interest. He said, "New York, eh? A little out of your territory, aren't you?"

Bolan replied, "I'm in grace. Just got here today."

"You better drop downtown in the morning and register. Is that a gun permit there? New York?"

"I'll be back over the line by midnight," Bolan assured him. He showed the cop the front side of the Ace of Spades, just for the hell of it.

Thompkins commented, "Consultant, huh? You must be a very busy man."

"I try to be," Bolan told him. "You're not going through this routine with every guy in the place, I hope."

"You want to read the warrant?"

The FBI guy was looking around, casing the layout.

Bolan told the big cop, "Let's be men. You boys must have better things to do, I'm sure. Go on. Get with it. Let's make this quick and easy."

"We'll need to talk to Stefano Angeletti."

"Does it say that in the warrant?"

"No. But I'm sure he'd like to cooperate. Oddly enough we have a common cause, I'm not exactly proud to say."

Bolan jerked a thumb toward the library and said, "He's in there. But it's getting late and he's tired. He's an old man, remember, and this is his doctor here." Bolan indicated Kastler with a twitch of the thumb. "It's been a tough day and I'm sure you know what I mean."

Thomkins said, *"You* are telling *me,"* and walked into the library.

Drasco and Kastler followed him in.

A younger plain-clothes cop stepped in from the outside, stared curiously at Bolan for a moment, then led the uniformed men into the big living room where the crews hung out.

Another troop moved in through the open doorway and went up the stairs to the second floor.

Bolan and the FBI guy were left alone in the reception hall.

The guy was giving him a very intent look. He cleared his throat and, in a very casual and low-pitched voice, told Bolan, "Brognola sends his regards."

Bolan's chest went ice cold and he tried to keep

his eyes and face the same as he replied, "Who?"

"He says it's a bad time for a hit."

Bolan let his lips slide into a lopsided, disbelieving grin. "Come on now," he said. "Not *you. Amicu di l'amici?*"

"Forget it and drop dead," the fed replied disgustedly and went on to the library.

Bolan watched him walk away. Under his breath he said, "Yeah, I almost did."

A loud commotion overhead at that moment brought the young plain-clothes cop hurrying from the crew room. Two uniformed men were retreating in confusion toward the stairway landing, accompanied by a variety of flying objects, some of which were crashing into the wall behind them and sending fragments of broken pottery and glass bouncing down to the main floor.

A young woman appeared at the top of the stairs, screaming vile words in an unending stream. She was clad only in bra and panties.

Frank the Kid ran into the hall and exclaimed, "Philippa!"

The young cop was starting up there.

Bolan jostled him aside, growled, "Let me," and led the way.

One of the uniformed officers told Bolan as he went past, "We have to look in that room."

Bolan said, "Sure you do. Come on."

He ducked a flying vase and scooped the woman up, carrying her back along the hallway under one arm. He called over his shoulder to the cops, "Get with it, let's go."

They went.

Philippa the Bitch was kicking and yelling and trying to bite a chunk out of Bolan's leg.

His free hand grabbed her by the hair of her head and he told her, "You're disgracing your papa. What's the matter with you, huh?"

She yelled, "I'm going to *kill* you, *all* of you!"

The young cop brushed past, gave Bolan a sympathetic smile, and went on to aid the men in blue.

Bolan recognized the cop. He'd spent a pleasant minute or so with the guy earlier that day.

The inspection upstairs took only another few seconds. The cops filed past, giving the man and his burden plenty of clearance; then Bolan carried the girl to her room and dropped her on the bed.

"Behave yourself," he said gently, and went out.

She was quiet now, sending a thoughtful gaze after him as he closed the door.

A guy down on the landing was reporting to another in the reception hall, "Nothing up there. It's clean."

The cops were leaving.

Another crisis was ending, another test met.

Others, however, were lying in wait for Mack the Wild Card. The night of tests had only just begun.

He flexed his shoulders, removed the tinted wire-frames and dropped them into the pocket, and went down to see what could be stirred up on this, his possibly last night on earth.

## Chapter 14/ *A Stirring*

Captain Thomkins held a brief meeting with his detail leaders just outside the entrance to the Angeletti property; shortly thereafter the army of cops began their decampment from the neighborhood.

The Captain himself, with FBI Agent Joseph Persicone in the vehicle with him, was among the first to take departure. He had the look of a man who would like nothing better than to simply let go and have a good, unembarrassed cry.

Persicone respected the mood until they were well clear of the area, then he broke the silence to admit, "That Cavaretta guy . . . for a minute there, for just one trembling moment, I had the creepy feeling that the guy was Mack Bolan.

"I just made an ass of myself. The guy thought I was trying to pose as an *amicu di l'amici*—a friend of the friends—a bought cop."

Thomkins grunted and commented, "You've been chasing the guy across too many towns, Joe. Glad I've just got the one. Few minutes ago you were trying to convince me he was blown to pieces."

"I know," Persicone said, sighing.

"Anyway, it just couldn't be. I know what that Cavaretta guy is. I'm going to run a make on him, just for the hell of it, but I already know. Did you notice his finger . . . tips? Sealed solid. He was sent down here by the old men in New York. And it was obvious that he was acting with plenty of authority. He was running the joint. Did you see the way he took over Philippa the Brat?"

"That was the young lady with tantrums? Yes, I caught the tail of it. Angeletti's daughter, eh?"

"The one and only."

Persicone said, "I gather she's not very popular with the official household. I caught a lot of sniggering and quiet cheering-on when Cavaretta grabbed her. Even old man Angeletti was whispering, 'Hit her, hit her.' Had to feel a bit sorry for the old guy. I'm Italian, you know. I know how he felt."

"Okay, Italian, tell me something I've often wondered about. How does the *girl* feel? Raised up in all that? She knows what her old man is, knows what he's done to get where he is. What's *her* place in all that?"

"She has no place," Persicone replied quietly. "Mafia or not, liberated twentieth century or not, the female members of a traditional Italian family have no place. They cook, they bear children, educate them, teach them to love the Holy Mother of God, and generally stand as the very center of the universe for their family. But they have no voice, no vote, not even any opinions in the affairs of their men. Worst of all, they even have to shed their tears in private."

"It's not still that way," Thomkins said. "Is it?"

"In a family like that one back there? Sure it is."

"It figures then," the Captain said. "Philippa's *fit*, I mean. I'd say she's about ready to blow a gas-

110

ket. That one is no shrinking madonna, I'll tell you."

"Could be," Persicone agreed. "I'll jot that down in my notes for future considerations. Unless Bolan makes future considerations unnecessary."

"What's your learned expert opinion in the matter?" the Captain growled. "Will the guy pop up again? Or is he through with our town."

"If he's not dead then he's not through," Persicone replied without even thinking about it.

"Well, he's not dead," Thompkins quietly declared.

"Then he's not through."

The Captain sighed. He stuck a cigarette between his lips and viciously jabbed his thumb against the dashboard lighter. "Neither am I," he said.

Persicone grinned. "What? No bottle and bedsprings?"

"Not until the guy is through," Thomkins growled.

"It's going to be a long night," Persicone said, sighing.

Thomkins lit his cigarette, expelled the smoke with a hiss, and said, "It's already been a long night. I left Strauss back there, though. He's young; he can take it."

"Take *what?*"

"The suspense. I put 'im on bird-dog stake-out. Told him not to come home until he's got the man by the throat."

"That could be dangerous . . . a man alone. . ."

"He's not all that alone. Three squads are back-

111

ing him up—way back but not so far away they can't give instant response."

"That's not a stake-out," Persicone said. "It's a forward scout at the enemy's door."

"That," said the get-Bolan chief, "is precisely what it is."


Stefano had gone up to "look in on" Philippa.

Doctor Kastler had taken his departure, leaving behind a supply of sedatives for both Philippa and Jules Sticatta.

Frank the Kid had found his own brand of sedatives at the library bar and it was obviously going to take a major disaster to blast him out of there in any foreseeable future.

Bolan/Cavaretta had taken a turn around the grounds to "hoorah" the troops out there, carrying a bottle of Frank's best bourbon for ambassadorial purposes, returning with an empty fifth and a lot of new friends.

He found Carmine Drasco huddled with his boys at a large card table near the TV set and dragged him off to the rear for "a kitchen conference".

It was all too obvious that Drasco held this "wild card" in the highest esteem. He was bursting with smug pride over this personal confab with the impressive storm trooper from New York and transparently anxious to make a good showing for himself.

Bolan watered that down immediately between gulps from a milk bottle at the refrigerator door.

"You're flat on your ass, Carmine," he told the guy. "We had you figured for too smart for this."

"I don't, uh, I don't get you, Johnny," Drasco replied in a rapidly deflating voice.

"I have better things to do with my time than to run around playing stink-finger with guys like this."

"What guys? I don't know—what's happened?"

"You tell *me* what's happened," Bolan bored on. "What's been happening in this crazy town all day, Carmine?"

"Well, God, it's been—hey, you just don't know. It's been sheer hell. One thing and another."

Bolan relented suddenly, smiling sympathetically and placing an arm around the *caporegime*'s shoulder to lead him toward the far corner of the room. His voice dropped to a near whisper as he said, "I know more than you think. Listen, why do you think I'm here?"

"Well, to—hell, Stefano said they were sending you to—you came to get Bolan off our backs, didn't you?"

"Has this Bolan been on your backs, Carmine?"

"You damn well know it! He took Cappy clear out of the picture early this morning. Then he hit us out at the Emperor's this afternoon like—well, you'd have to be there to know like what. He—"

"Did you *see* the boy, Carmine?"

"What boy? Who, *Bolan?* Of course I. . ."

"Did you *see* him? With your own two eyes?"

"Well . . . I guess I didn't. But somebody sure as hell did. He left about thirty dead men behind who I guess saw him." The Southy lieutenant had been whispering. He raised his voice to inquire, "What the hell are we whispering for?"

"You either go on like you were or shut up!" Bolan hissed back. "This whole damn place might have ears. Listen! What makes you think it was Bolan at the Emperor's today?"

"What makes me *think*. . . ? Are you saying . . . ? I don't get this, Johnny. What the hell are you telling me?"

Bolan pushed him deeper into the corner. "Look," he said, "I don't belong to any family. You know? Like a guy living in the District of Columbia—right? He has no allegiance to any *state*. Right? That's me, Carmine. And that's my boss. And my boss tells me *this*, Carmine. He says, 'Do what you can, Johnny. Talk to those boys down there in Philly, but talk to them quietly. And don't you do a thing else until we get all this cleared through council.' "

"All this *what?*" the guy wailed.

"All this, you know." Bolan rolled his eyes, shrugged his shoulders, patted his chest, and dropped his gaze to the floor.

Carmine Drasco was in danger of popping several blood veins in his face and throat. His eyes were shifting violently from side to side and his breath was coming in stuttering gasps. He half-whispered, half-shouted, "What the hell are you telling me?"

"I'm not telling you anything," Bolan/Cavaretta quietly assured him, the tone a sombre *sotto voce*. "But I'm going to *show* you something, Carmine. After that, what you decide is your own business. Like I said, I have to stay neutral. I have to stay that way until somebody way upstairs says otherwise. You know?"

Carmine Drasco obviously "knew".

After all, it had been a most difficult day in Philadelphia. A day to believe almost anything. At this point, Drasco was ready to believe most anything.

Johnny Cavaretta was being one hell of a nice guy, letting Carmine in on something earth-shaking. It had to be . . . and, yeah, Carmine Drasco was ready to buy everything.

He was not quite prepared, however, for what Bolan/Cavaretta had stashed away in the luggage compartment of the Maserati.

Bolan led him out there without a word, snapped open the lid, and told the guy, "See what there is to see. But—on your sacred blood, Carmine —not a word, not a Goddamned word to anybody."

Carmine looked, and his eyes boggled at what they beheld. He reached in for a feel, patted the lifeless face, then spat on it.

Bolan pushed him away and closed the exhibit, then dragged the muted, almost staggering *caporegime* back into the house.

Drasco dropped into a chair and passed a quivering hand across his face. He said, "I don't get—I guess I don't—how long has that been in there, Johnny?"

"Since about noon today," Bolan/Cavaretta lied without a qualm.

"Well, okay, I—yeah . . . I guess I had it figured for something like that, from what you . . . I mean. . ."

115

The guy was all torn up, pinned cruelly upon the horns of both joy and wriggling fear.

Bolan prodded that latter emotion a bit. "Like I said, Carmine. I'd *show* you something. After that it's up to you."

"But if you bagged the guy about noon . . . then . . . well, wait a minute, now. Who . . . ?"

Bolan nodded his head and gave the guy a sober wink. "Exactly," he said. "Who hit the Emperor's?"

"Well, I'm damned if I know," Drasco declared raggedly. "I didn't see *anything,* to tell the truth." His eyes flared suddenly and he yelled, "Hey!" He staggered off the chair, pivoted toward the door to the crew room and cried, "That rotten *fink!*"

"What rotten fink?" Bolan asked quietly.

"He kept saying he *saw* him, he *saw* him—clear as day and big as a mountain, that's what he said! And that little *bitch!* She *hit* him, she said! Imagine that! I thought she was just . . . kept saying it over and over, she *hit* him! Jesus Christ, what a fucking sap I been! Poor old Jules, Goddamned near cremated!"

Drasco spun about to show Bolan a tortured, betrayed and utterly demoralized loyal liege to the chief. He was almost sobbing as he asked, "Why would he do that, Johnny?"

Bolan felt like a bastard for sure and he did not have to fake the sadness as he replied, "Because he's dying, that's why. An old man sometimes gets desperate, especially when things are untidy behind him. Don't blame him too much."

"Naw, you got the wrong slant on it. It wasn't Stefano. It was that fink of a kid, fucked-up Frank,

116

the ninety-second wonder. Those were *his* boys, his *wops*—and he even knocked off a bunch of them just to get to us! What d' you think of a kid what would hit his own papa?"

"And can't even do *that* right," Bolan added.

"He sure didn't! All he got was a bunch of his own wops and a piece of poor old Jules. That rotten—I'm gonna—"

Bolan grabbed the guy and jerked him back as he lunged toward the crew-room door. "You're doing nothing!" he said coldly. "Don't you worry, it's already in council. That's why I'm here."

"Well, dammit, what'm I supposed to do, just *sit* here and *smile* about it?"

"I'm just going to tell you what I would do, Carmine. I leave the rest up to you. If it was me, I'd take Jules home, I mean straight home. He's hurting and he needs to be home. I'd do that first. Then I'd round up all his *regime;* I'd get them hard and I'd tell them to shoot the first greaser that crossed the line. Then I'd go home and do the same for my own, and I'd sit tight and let Johnny Cavaretta do his own job his own way."

Drasco's gaze was darting about the kitchen. He was thinking—*survival* thinking. Presently he asked, "What about Stefano?"

"Johnny Cavaretta is here with Stefano, Carmine."

Drasco was huffing and puffing and still thinking about it.

Bolan lit a cigarette and passed it to him.

The guy huffed some more, ignoring the cigarette, then said, "That's why you're here?"

117

"It's exactly why I'm here. I didn't even have to come to Philly otherwise. I bagged my game over in Jersey."

Drasco had come to his decision. He grabbed Bolan's hand and pumped it throughout the long speech. "I want you to know, Johnny, and I want you to tell all our dear friends in New York, that this is the nicest thing anybody has ever did for me. I mean that from the bottom of my heart. All these years with Stefano and he never done nothing like this for Carmine Drasco. He even sat on his tail once't and let Cappy horn right into my territory without no explanation—not even a by-your-leave. Not even, no, not a gentle cough to warn me. I mean it, I'll never forget this, Johnny."

Bolan the Dirty Bastard told him, "I'm sure you won't, Carmine."

Five minutes later, Drasco and all his boys plus the heavily sedated Jules Sticatta were off the property and huffing their way home.

Wild Card Bolan sent with them his blessings. He would do all in his power to help them huff their houses down. He and Frank the Kid and all his beloved *gradigghia.*

## Chapter 15/ *Requiem For an Empire*

Bolan passed the word to his new dear friend, the yard boss, that no one—but *no* one—came onto that property without Johnny Cavaretta's personal approval. Then he went to find Don Stefano, and found him at his desk, glaring sourly at his kid and heir, who was by now finding it quite an achievement to merely maintain equilibrium atop a barstool.

The old man turned around with a sigh and told the Executioner, "I should've had a kid like you, Johnny."

"Give him time, Steven," Bolan replied, using the surname reserved for the use of *capi* and other stellars of the organization. "He might surprise you yet."

"Not tonight, I guess," the old Don said.

"Does he do this often?" Bolan asked.

"No, usually he just runs and sticks his dick in some cheap broad. Tonight the bar just happened to be handier."

Bolan chuckled. "You're too hard on him maybe."

"Hard my ass," Angeletti sneered. "I give him everything and he turns it all to dust."

"Whoever gave *you* anything, Steven?" Bolan asked gently.

"Huh? Nobody ever game *me* a damned—oh! I

see where you're getting. Well, maybe that's right. I thought about that too."

Bolan broke a lengthening silence to report, "I shuffled the hard defenses. And I sent Jules and Carmine home."

A vein popped in the old man's neck and he stiffened in his chair as he protested, "I told them to stay here with—where do you get off telling my boys where to go and when to go?"

"Hey, they got things to protect too," Bolan reminded the boss of Philly. "This isn't the only place in town the guy could decide to hit. You have all the protection you'll need. Relax and let me take care of it."

"*You* relax!" the old man yelled. "It's *my* hide, don't tell *me* to relax!"

"There's a hundred cops out there," Bolan argued. "You're paying taxes. Get a little back."

"I thought they'd gone," the old man said, easing off a bit.

Bolan chuckled. "They're not gone far. Don't worry. That guy won't get within sight of this joint tonight. And if he does. . ." Bolan slapped an imaginary figure in space with the heel of his hand. ". . . right into the trap and off with his head. You got to have more respect for the law in your town, Steven."

The old man cackled and reached for a cigar. Bolan lit it for him and told him, "There's not many like you left, Steven."

"I 'preciate you saying that, Johnny. Because I respect you, too. I know what you can do . . . what you've done. That job in Jersey last month was, well, I mean, that was the neatest I ever saw, and I've seen some."

Bolan said, "It's great of you to say that. I guess we got quite a thing going, you and me." He laughed. "Too bad you're not forty years younger and split-tailed."

The old man thought that statement a riot. He laughed until he choked, had to sip some wine, pounded the desk for a full half-minute, then slyly reminded his guest, "I know somebody named Angeletti fills that bill to a tee—and its name ain't *Frank*."

Bolan laughed and held up both hands. "Oh hey, don't matchmake *me*, Steven. I'm nowhere near my quota yet."

"Well, you could do worse," Angeletti said, maybe a bit more than half serious. "And I'll bet she'd never give *you* any shit, I'll bet that."

Bolan said, "I'll keep that in mind."

"You should. I, uh, to tell the truth, Johnny. . ."

Bolan prompted him. "I'm always ready for the truth, Steven."

The clouded old eyes flicked toward the bar. The voice dropped as he confided, "I've about given up on Frank. I mean . . . let's be men, Johnny. The kid just never is going to have it. And I—"

Bolan cut him off with a wave of the hand. His face screwed into a troubled frown as he told Don Stefano, "Please—Steven, please. Let's don't discuss that. Nothing about that. I mean . . . I sympathize, I know the problem . . . but I'm too close to it and I. . ."

The old man was perched there on the edge of his chair, giving Bolan the Bastard a quizzical, searching scan of the eyes. "I don't, uh, I don't get you, Johnny. You're too close to *what?*"

"Let's just drop it."

"Drop it my ass! Now, come on!"

Bolan smiled soberly and said, "We have a thing, you and me. Right? Let's leave it that way, and never any hard feelings. Never you having to say that you sat right in my face and discussed this with Johnny Cavaretta and he never gave you a thing, not a tumble. Spare me that, Steven."

"Well, now wait. I respect your . . . I wouldn't want to press a friendship, Johnny. But if there's something I ought to know, then I ought to know it. You can't do this, Johnny. You can't come in here and drop something like that, then just clam up. I mean, I pledge to you, on my solemn word and sacred blood, I'm telling you that I would never—no, never would I rat on a confidence from a friend."

Bolan stared at him for a long moment, then dropped his eyes, stretched his neck and said, "I'm not telling you this, Steven. I wouldn't ever tell a man I respect as much as I respect you that his heir problems are over."

"What?"

"I just couldn't say something like that to a man who has done so much in this outfit. For so many years. I mean . . . I couldn't. Not even if I'd been sitting right there at the table when the problem got resolved, I still couldn't say a word."

Don Stefano re-lit his cigar. The hands trembled. He sipped his wine and the hands trembled worse.

"When were you sitting at that table, Johnny?" he asked, the voice hardly more than a sigh.

"I shouldn't say, Steven. Please."

"Today? Was it today?"

Bolan fingered the tape at his jaw. "I only *got* to New York today. I been up in the country for nearly a month, ever since that Jersey job."

"I see." The old man was obviously seeing quite a bit. He said, "Thank you, Johnny. One more thing. In strictest confidence. Look, I'm an old man. What could I do? What *would* I do? After all these years of loyalty, would I buck the outfit? What they want is what I want. But I got a right to know. After all these years. I got a right. What are they talking about doing to me, Johnny?"

Bolan hesitated, giving the moment its most dramatic play, then he sighed and told the old man, "Not just *talking*, Steven."

"So . . . what? Huh? Dammit, *what?*

"Why did they tell you I was coming here, Steven?"

"Well I—well, they—we couldn't talk right out. He just said he was sending me some *help*."

"Some help to do what?"

"Well, this damned Bolan shit, what d'you think? Isn't that what they meant?"

"Did he say anything about some delegations coming down? Some boys from upstate? Some boys from New York downtown?"

"What are you saying? Why *did* you come, Johnny?"

Bolan's glance slid to Frank the Kid, wobbling half off his stool. He said, "God, I hate to be the one to tell you this, Steven."

"Let's be men, Johnny!"

"Okay." Bolan's chin came up. He fixed the old man with a cold, hard stare and told him, "Things just can't get to *that*, Steven." The gaze flicked to Frank the Kid and back to Papa. "Do you understand me? You wouldn't firm it up for yourself, so they firmed it up for you. They're not waiting, Steven. They're not waiting for you to die. Not with Frank the Fuck-up and a hundred greasers backing him up. They say there will be blood in the streets, money down the sewer and hell to pay all over this land, Steven. It's the sort of thing that keeps people like me so busy all the time. And they just can't have it. They will not have it, Steven."

A long silence ensued.

Angeletti played with his cigar, toyed with his wine, smacked his lips, looked at Frank, looked at the Wild Card from New York who'd brought him such distressing news, smacked his lips some more then sighed, "Well, I'm damned if they will."

"You promised me, Steven."

"I'd promise you hell, Johnny. But I won't give you my only kid."

"There's always Philippa."

"That *slut?*"

"Now, now."

"You can't have him, Johnny."

"I didn't come for him, Steven."

"Then, what *did* you come for?"

"If you'd like to take a little walk, I'll show you."

That old chin dropped and both hands crawled along the desk. Aghast, he asked, "*Me,* Johnny?"

'Oh, God, no, don't even think that. What I came for, I already have. It's in the car. If you want to go see, okay. If not, forget it. Makes no difference. But don't think . . . aw, hell, Steven, don't think. . ."

"I don't think I want to go out there in the dark with you, Johnny."

"All your boys are out there. *Your* boys, not mine." Bolan reached for the wallet and the old man jumped a foot. "Hey, easy, I *told* you, don't even think . . . here."

He tossed the letter of credit from Cavaretta's wallet across the desk.

"Note the date on there. It's today. Look where it came from. Atlanta, Georgia—right? How did it get clear up here, so fast? It flew, by special courier. It flew to me, Steven. Look at the amount. Fifty gee, right? I picked it up right down here at North Philly Airport at two o'clock today. *Two* o'clock, Steven. Now. If you'll just walk out to the car with me, dammit, I'll show you how I earned that."

The old man's curiosity was definitely aroused. He sniffed and pushed the letter back across the desk, then slowly got to his feet.

"Show me," he commanded.

A minute and a half later, Bolan showed him.

Angeletti had to feel the face, manipulate the stiffening arms and legs, examine the weapons.

He said, "So that's the guy."

"That *was* him," Bolan said.

Stefano spun about suddenly and went back into the house. Bolan closed the exhibit for the second time and followed the Don inside.

At the library door, Angeletti asked him, "What does it all mean? You say you got paid at two o'clock. I say I got hit by the guy at about six. What does it mean?"

"It means somebody's playing games with you, Steven."

"Who?"

"Who did they say was coming down?"

Marble lips replied, "Delegation from Buffalo, two from the city."

"There you go. Maybe they got here early."

"Maybe they did." All of the old man's starch had deserted him. "I'm going to bed. I don't feel so hot. I thought that was too much for one lousy guy, I knew it was too much. I'm old. I'm tired. I'm going to bed. I respect you, Johnny. For this, I mean. Thanks."

"Let me tell you this, Steven. It will make you sleep better. There was a split decision. Understand? A *split* decision. Some said yes, some said no. Until that's finally talked out, Mike says we step in. Right? Understand me? *We* step in, Steven."

"I'm glad to hear that. Just tell me this. Was Augie saying yes or saying no."

"Augie was saying no."

"God, I'm glad to hear that. You're here to, uh, see that the *yeses* pull back their horns. Is that it?"

"That's about it, Steven. Go on to bed. Don't worry. Let me handle it."

"Put the kid to bed, will you?"

126

"You know I will. Now, you put yourself there."

"I wish to God I'd had a kid like *you*, Johnny."

Bolan had to turn away from that and clear his mind of that pathetic sick old face.

He had to remind himself that the melody played by ear was not always the one a guy would choose for himself if there had been a choice.

For a moment—for one tumbling instant—he debated going out there and climbing in that forty-thousand-dollar shark and simply driving the hell away from that place.

But . . . if he did that . . . what would have been accomplished in Philadelphia? What good all the dead, what good all the extra pressure and expense on a city already overburdened with her share of problems . . . what good any of it?

The Executioner had not come to Philadelphia for a split decision.

He had come for a knockout.

So, at the end of that tumbling moment of hesitation, Bolan reminded himself that there was no morality in warfare, no right and no wrong to any of it.

You had to hit them where you could, and drop them where they stood.

Even soul-sick, dying old men.

## Chapter 16/ *The Mark*

Bolan had never regarded himself as a superior strategist nor as a genius at anything. He simply made use of what he had, and kept trying.

He knew that he could not have set up the Angeletti family for this sort of an inside knockover with any amount of genius or planning. It was daring, sure, and fraught with mortal consequences with every move, every word, every action. But that was what life had been for Mack Bolan ever since the beginning of his home-front war. And he could not have set the family up that way had the stage itself not already been well prepared by circumstances far beyond any one man's control or manipulation.

He had simply barged in and played his game upon their stage.

It was as simple as that.

And it was quite a stage the mob had built for themselves. Constructed of rotting timbers upon unreliable foundations, erected with lust and malice, well-garnished with deceit, dishonesty, and a callous disregard for the essential nobility of mankind—it was a veritable hall of horrors, even for those who misspent their lifetimes strutting before its footlights.

Yes, it was quite a setting for any maestro who had the nerve to leap into the orchestra pit and strike up a funeral dirge.

*Nerve*, probably—in the final analysis—was Mack Bolan's chief stock in trade. And the market, in Philadelphia, was definitely bullish.

This was Bolan's own understanding of himself and of his task. Perhaps, however, he was too modest in his evaluations of self.

Perhaps there was a spark of greatness to the man, an effervescent *something* at the base of his being that just instinctively turned him into the right word at the crucial time, the proper deed at the intersection with its need.

None would deny that Mack Bolan had been "as good as dead" at that very moment when a police spotlight pinned him to an overhead perch, defenseless, within shouting distance of his enemy's stronghold.

Few would have given him any edge for survival, afoot and surrounded by hostile forces of overwhelming superiority, even after his miraculous escape from that stunning confrontation with the law.

One or two, perhaps, would have guessed that he might seek refuge in the most unlikely spot—the enemy's camp.

But none in God's green world would have dared to predict that this desperate fugitive, within minutes after penetrating that enemy stronghold, would have seized upon his own stark misfortune and jeopardy to mold of it the grand-slam knockout punch that would rattle not only Philadelphia, but be experienced around the Mafia world.

It was precisely what he was attempting.

And perhaps Mack Bolan was not exactly a new

idea in that cosmic experiment called mankind.

From an ancient Chinese military manual (c.500 B.C.):

> The mark of greatness is upon that general who, through daring and resourcefulness, rescues resounding victory from certain disaster.

And, yes—who knows? Maybe "the universe" *does* reserve a special place here and there for men such as these.

Had Mack Bolan asked the question, he would have his answer within a short few hours.

But he hadn't asked. He was simply trying. It was the mark of Bolan.

Bolan sent the house captain upstairs to keep vigil outside Don Stefano's bedroom door and he gave the other two inside boys to Sammy, the yard boss.

This left Bolan alone, downstairs, with Frank the Kid, who was passed out on the bar.

He went exploring, and found a music room or something adjoining the library at the bar end. There was a concert grand piano in there, a harp—a real, honest-to-God harp—that stood taller than Bolan, shelves piled with well-indexed sheet music and, in the back corner, a twentieth-century marvel which was a stereo theatre built into a cast-form plastic chair, made like a big bubble and looking a bit like a small helicopter's cabin, comfortable-looking padded seat, console, the whole bit. A neat stack of classical LP albums completed the picture —and somehow none of it fit the image of anyone whom Bolan had seen in the joint so far.

A record on the turntable attracted his attention —the label, mainly. It was pale lavender and had no distributor's tag on it. Printed on that label, though, was the answer to the entire room. The record, obviously privately cut, was tagged simply: Phil Angeletti, *Private Moods for Concert Piano.*

The find was quite a revelation. Bolan idly started it going, listened to the first minute or so, then stopped it. He was no impresario, but it sounded damn good to him. Who would have thought it of Philippa the Bitch?

He went out of there, then, and continued the exploration, finding that which he sought a couple of minutes later; a doorway off the kitchen led to a darkened stairway and a basement room—a crew room with six bunks in it, small refrigerator and hotplate, table and four chairs.

Beyond that and past a door about a foot thick was a pistol range, well lighted, probably acoustically engineered and soundproofed. At the far end were regular target pits and four steel targets in human form. One of these targets was wearing a blacksuit similar to Bolan's. It was bullet-riddled and torn half off the target.

Bolan bit his teeth and went out of there.

It was a little before eight o'clock when Bolan helped Frank the Kid upstairs and to his bedroom. He steered him on to the bath, bent him over the toilet, stuck a finger down his throat and urged up everything in the guy's stomach.

Then he washed his face with cold water and put him to bed fully clothed.

The guy was still out of it, marginally conscious, babbling something in the old tongue.

Booze, Bolan knew, often talked—but never in its own words. It merely released those which were ordinarily repressed by a more prudent consciousness.

He patted the Kid's face with a cold towel and growled, "Talk American, dammit."

"Agrigento . . . told 'em . . . hell . . . the *best,*

see . . . hell's coming and we *got* to. Don Cafu, *fuck* that guy . . . I told 'em, I told 'em. . . ."

"*Gradigghia*," Bolan prompted.

"Damn right, I told 'em. All or nothing. But . . . *shit!*"

"What'd you say about Agrigento?" It was a Sicilian province, one of the early homes of the Mafia.

"Don Cafu says a thousand a day. Can you beat that? A *day?*" The guy sniggered, choked, retched —Bolan yanked his head to the side of the bed and he vomited some more, onto the floor.

The interrogation went on, Bolan patiently probing through alcohol-wreathed mutterings and mumblings and retchings. It ended ten minutes later with the guy bawling his heart out and promising over and over to do better next time.

Bolan quietly assured him that he would, and left him with his heartbreak.

He rapped lightly on the door to Philippa's room and went in.

She was sitting up in bed, pillows plumped behind her, gazing broodingly at a small, personal-sized bedside television.

She looked up briefly at his entrance, then returned her visual attention to the TV. "Privacy," she said in a low, unemotional tone. "That's what I like about this house, the total privacy."

"Put some locks on the doors," Bolan suggested.

"Put in a word to Papa on that, will you?" she replied acidly.

She was not looking at him, not yet.

Bolan moved a chair to the bed, lowered himself

into it, relaxed, lit a cigarette. He knew immediately that he'd done the wrong thing. It was the first relaxed moment he'd had all day, and it all came out—all the stress, all the vital systems too highly peaked for too damn long, all the small physical damages overlooked and awaiting their proper share of attention.

He was bushed.

His stomach growled and clutched at its neglect.

Overused and abused arms and legs ached. A dull throb was finding room to play at the back of his neck and along the base of the skull. Hot little twinges told of raw places in the flesh of his chest and shoulders.

In that moment of self-awareness, he also found a new awareness of the girl. She didn't look her thirty-two years, except where her mad showed through. She was wearing a frilly pink bedjacket with silk roses closing the front of it . . . and she looked great. Bolan was reminded once again that Italian women are among the world's most beautiful.

She switched off the television with a jerk and turned to the unbidden visitor with a sigh. "Did you come in here just to stare holes through me?" she asked him.

He replied, "No. I came in to relax a moment with the pretty lady who plays a *hell* of a mean piano."

She looked flustered, then smiled and told him, "You look tired."

"I am tired."

"Want a drink?"

He shook his head. "That would lay me out for sure. Okay if I call you Phil?"

She said, "Hear, hear. The man is asking, not telling."

"I played one of your records without asking, too. Sounded great. I'll bet you could make a living out of that."

She said, "There's another word to put in on Papa."

He told her, "No need to. Phil, you need to leave this house."

"I needed to leave this house ten years ago," she replied in a flat voice. "Make that twenty."

"Shut up, I'm serious."

She blinked oversized eyes at him several times, then told him, "We really are in trouble, then."

"You know it."

"What's going on? Who *are* you? Where is—?"

He cut in with, "Hell is going on. Who I am isn't important. What I want *is*. I want you out of here. Tonight."

Her eyes inspected the blank television screen for a moment before she replied, "It's not much, but it's home. The only home I have. I'm not leaving it."

"Grow up," he said tiredly. "And get out."

They were his parting words. He left her with perplexity and silent curiosity surging across that pretty face. He went out of there.

The house captain nodded to him from the little alcove which led to the Don's bedroom. Bolan went down there and asked the guy, "What time is it?"

"It's eight, uh, seventeen."

"At ten seventeen you make sure I'm on my feet and wide awake," Bolan commanded.

"Yessir. Where will you be?"

"Where will an empty bed be?"

The captain smiled and pointed to a door halfway along the hall. "There's one in there."

"Then, that's where I'll be," Bolan told him, and went there.

The spare bedroom smelled musty and long unused. A small bath adjoined. The furnishings were simple but adequate—clean. Bolan opened the lone window and brought fresh air inside, then leaned out to orient himself. It was a back room, but angled to the regular lines of the house. The carport was directly below at ninty degrees. He could see the north and west walls from the window, now and then a moving shadow as yardmen patrolled.

What, he wondered, the hell was he doing *here?*

He was, he answered himself with a tired sigh, preparing to take a shower and lie down for a nap in the enemy's camp.

Standing in, he darkly reflected, for a lump of clay that was slowly turning to dust in the trunk of that car down there.

And standing out, like a clay pigeon, for the first thing that came in off the numbers.

And for *what?*

It was all looking so damn hopeless. Not the battle, but the war.

The interrogation of Frank the Kid was responsible for Bolan's dark mood. If it hadn't been wild ravings, not merely booze talk, then the American underworld was setting up a *massive* transfusion of "new blood" for itself.

According to Frank, a guy called Don Cafu—in the Sicilian province of Agrigento—was conscripting armies and offering them as a package deal on an open market, with a going rate of one thousand American dollars per day per *gradigghia*.

On an annual basis, that could tote up to quite a sum. Considering the fantastic profits from organized crime, however, a 365 thou' annual investment for "security" would be peanuts to most bosses.

And just look at all the peace of mind those peanuts could buy!

Dammit! He *had* to stop that.

But how?

The answer seemed to lie at his finger tips, all about him. He had to stop, first, the Angeletti experiment in imported armies. If he lived beyond that, then . . . well, Bolan had learned to take it one fight at a time, day by day, heartbeat by heartbeat.

The war he had to win and *keep* winning was the war of *right here and now*.

But . . . right here and now he was running quickly out of gas and he was preparing to lie down in the valley of the shadow of death, in the presence of his enemies.

## Chapter 18/ *The New Deck*

He was nude from the waist up, a sheet pulled up over his trousers and riding the hips, the Browning auto in his right fist and nuzzling the thigh beneath the sheet.

The eyes were half-closed and he appeared to be asleep, the respiration slow and even, body relaxed; actually he was in that light stage of consciousness which he referred to as "combat sleep" —hovering in complete physical and mental relaxation, the intellect submerged, but some animal edge of mind alert and aware of the world about him.

He knew when the door opened and he sensed the presence beside the bed.

The eyes flicked full open and the Browning's saftey clicked free at the same instant; otherwise he had not moved.

Philippa reacted as though he had sat bolt upright and yelled at her, however. She rebounded a couple of backward steps and gasped something silly. "I—I thought you were awake," she said, as though she'd come in and found him sound asleep and oblivious to her presence.

Her eyes fled to the lighted lamp at the other side of the bed as she amended the statement. "I mean, when I first came in."

She was dressed for going, in a clingy knit pants suit with hugely flared legs. A floppy hat was perched atop her head and she was holding a cosmetic travel case.

Bolan had still not moved; he did so now, stowing the Browning in the leather which hung on the bedpost at his right shoulder and glancing at his watch. The time was nine-five. He remained on the bed and told her, "You're leaving—good."

Philippa the Woman was staring at the blue blotches across his torso and upper arms. She perched tensely on the edge of the bed and asked him, "How many cattle were in the stampede?"

He growled, "What stampede?"

"The one that stomped all over that lovely body."

She would have never believed the truth even if he'd been inclined to give it to her. He grinned sourly and told her, "Little accident. Looks worse than it feels."

"The captain told me who you are. Guess I should have known." She sighed. "Funny. I ran across two truly impressive men today. One I shot at. The other I threw a vase at." She smiled and wrinkled her nose. "Story of my life."

"Maybe things are looking up," he murmured. "Right outside these walls I'll bet you'll find piles of impressive men."

"Well . . . I wanted to apologize."

"For what?"

"For trying to conk you."

He said, "Apology noted and accepted."

She moved a hand onto the bare chest and lightly explored the universe's bruises with careful finger tips. The exploration paused here and there at some little red lumps which seemed to stand apart from the other discolorations. An indefinable emotion momentarily clouded those bright eyes and she told him, "Frank got mad at me once when I was a little girl—oh, lots of times—but once he grabbed up his air rifle and let me have it, three times right across my tummy. The B-B's made marks on me just like these." She encircled one of the red lumps on Bolan's chest. "Has someone been shooting at you with an air rifle?"

Bolan knew what was bothering her—and he knew, suddenly, that she was the one who'd unloaded the shotgun at him from that upstairs window at the Emperor's.

He told her, "Shotgun pellets make the same mark if they don't penetrate. I know. I was a kid once, too." He forced a laugh and managed to make it sound real. "I've had a lot of buckshot picked out of my tail."

"Yes, that's what it looks like," she said, frowning.

He asked her, hoping to change the subject, "Did you come in to say good-bye, or what?"

She wrinkled her nose at him, the wounds apparently forgotten, and replied, "Or what. Captain tells me you'll have to okay my release. At the gate. No one comes or goes without your approval. My, how important you are!"

He said, "Oh," and slid out the back side of the bed to perch in the open window. He called down, "Sammy!"

He heard the word being passed across the grounds. Presently the yard boss was standing beneath the window, gazing up at him. He told the guy, "Miss Angeletti is going out. It's okay."

"Okay. Hey, I was just coming in to tell you. Three cars of boys are out there. Say they were sent. Do I let them in?"

Bolan replied, "Not yet." He turned to the woman and told her, "You'd better truck. That hell I mentioned just showed up."

Then he instructed the yard boss, "Get it on up here. Quick!"

Philippa was at the doorway and moving when he pulled his head back inside. He called after her, "Stay gone awhile!"

Her voice, half-angered, floated back from the hallway, "I'm never coming back."

Bolan snatched up his shirt, muttered, "Good for you," and hurriedly dressed. The brief rest had helped. The danger of the unknown which awaited at that gate helped much more, and the Executioner was now *all systems go*.

He was snugging into the gun-leather when Sammy, the yard boss, huffed into the room. Bolan pushed him back into the hall, telling him, "Come on."

The house captain was helping Philippa with some luggage. Bolan ordered him to "See her clear to the gate and the hell out of here!" Then he and Sammy barged into the Don's bedroom.

It looked like a hospital room and smelled like one. The bedside table was littered with medicines and illuminated by a reddish nightlight. The old man was propped up in a bed which could be ele-

141

vated at either end. He was sleeping with shuddering snores.

The eyes flipped open at Bolan's touch, however, and the voice sounded alert and knowing as the Don asked, "What's up?"

"Those delegations are standing at the gate," Bolan reported. "Three carloads."

"So I thought you were handling it."

"We weren't expecting them here tonight. Not *here*. I don't know for sure just *who* is out there and I don't know for sure if they'll listen to me. How do you feel about fifty-fifty risks?"

"Fifty-fifty is sucker's odds," the old man said. "Right."

"But . . . Johnny, I don't want no gunfights around here if we can help it."

"My feelings exactly," Bolan truthfully replied. "The cops would love to pounce in here and haul us all off to jail. We have to handle it without a fight. You want to risk that?"

"I'm getting too old to risk anything, Johnny. What do you suggest?"

"Well . . . I always believed in facing one crisis at a time."

"What does that mean?"

"Look . . . Steven . . . we both know why those boys are here. I don't think they'll listen to me. I don't think they'll even *know* me. But what I have to suggest is . . . well, it's really beyond my authority."

"You're backing off!" the old man sneered.

"The hell I am. I'm just telling you where I stand. Sammy here is *your* boy, not mine. I can't

142

tell him to let those cars in one at a time and to take those crews down to the basement one at a time. I can't tell him to—"

Angeletti stopped the "suggestion" with a wave of the hand. "We know how to handle it," he snapped. "Sammy!"

"Yessir, I'm right here."

"You're in charge of this. You remember how we handled the German boys."

"Yessir."

"Okay. You put a couple of boys down there in the pits, with choppers. Unscrew the light bulbs back there so it's dark when you turn the other lights on."

Bolan/Cavaretta suggested, "You'll want to use a Judas goat."

"Right," the old man agreed. "Use one of your smallest boys, a boy who can fall into that trench on the side."

Bolan said, "You also need to make them think you're still dumb. But you're taking no chances. You know? Crazy things have been happening around here and you want them inside—one car at a time. Now, they won't surrender their hardware, we all know that. But we don't want any gun play that's going to be heard. You're getting 'em back to the carports, then you're taking them inside for a drink. Only you take them downstairs; that's where the meeting is. You know?"

Sammy the yard boss knew. He went out, grim-lipped and ready to do-or-die for his *Capo*.

Bolan told Sammy's *Capo*: "That's a hell of a boy you've got there."

143

"The very best," Angeletti agreed. "He's done this before. He knows how. You know what this means though, Johnny. It's a war."

That was, Bolan darkly reflected, precisely what it was.

With the enemy engaging itself.

## Chapter 19/ *The Count*

Bolan waited upstairs until the house captain returned from his errand with the departing *bambina*; then he grabbed the guy and ordered him to awaken Frank.

"Keep him up here out of the way, though," Bolan added. "And sober him up. I don't care what you have to do. Dunk him in the bathtub, beat the shit out of him, I don't care. But get him sober."

The look in the captain's eyes indicated that he would relish that assignment. He went happily into the Kid's room and Bolan returned to the bedroom he'd used, picked up the tinted-lens glasses he'd worn earlier that evening, and went down the stairs in his shirtsleeves—the shoulder/chest rig with the Browning on open display.

He went to the library to rummage for cigarettes, found an open pack of Marlboro's on the bar, lit one and went on to the kitchen.

There he found hard bread and cheese and the remnants of the milk he'd sampled earlier. As he fed biological demands of his body, his mind dwelt on different food.

It was very clear in his mind . . . that scene below. The visiting gun crews would be led down the stairs, through the ready room down there, and into the pistol range.

The "Judas goat" would be chattering at them as he brought them in for slaughter, joking or wisecracking about the super-security of this crazy night in Philadelphia. He would flip on the lights and make a dive for cover as the heavy door banged shut behind them.

At that instant, before the victims could even have a clear idea of where they were, two or three submachine guns would open up from the target pits back there in the darkness. That soundproofed room would be filled with a withering hail of death on the wing, and another group of strutters from the hall of horrors would find the curtain ringing down on their final performance before the footlights of the House of Mafia—and they would die as they had lived, angrily, profanely, stupidly.

Then the Judas goat would brush himself off, help conceal the bloodied carcasses of his former *amici,* and strut up to bring in another troupe.

Bolan sighed and left much of his snack untouched, went instead to the screened porch and smoked in a corner, arms folded across his chest, waiting.

The first crew wagon eased in, lights off, Sammy the yard boss walking alongside, yamming it up with the driver. The vehicle halted just outside the carport; doors opened, nine men unwound themselves from confinement and staggered around getting their legs under them.

Someone out there declared in a tired voice, "First of all, I got to take a piss."

Someone else said, "It's awful quiet around here. Thought you was havin' a war."

Sammy was telling them, "We got everything waiting for you right inside. Just go on in. Here,

146

Tommy Dukes will show you the way. It's down-stairs, that's where we're getting it together. Hey . . . chow, some drinks maybe while we put it together, eh?"

Bolan was watching, searching faces as they moved into the light from the house.

He stiffened suddenly, his face going to stone, and he hung the tinted lenses across his face.

The guys were coming on in twos and threes, small-talking and adjusting to a straggly single file as they approached the door.

Sammy had stepped in ahead of them, was ushering them through with chummy remarks. Bolan moved up behind him and quietly commanded, "Cut one out for me, I'll want some words. This guy just coming in—naw, make it the next one. He looks like a honcho or something."

"He is," Sammy agreed, and moved to intercept the guy.

Bolan retired to his corner, arms folded, smoking, watching.

Sammy the yard boss had *Leo Turrin* by the arm, telling him something and pulling him out of the procession.

A thumb jerked toward Bolan and Leo the Pussy tossed a curious glance that way.

Without changing position or expression, Bolan called over, "The library, Sammy."

The yard boss gave directions; Leo was staring curiously at the tall figure in the corner as he moved into the hallways and disappeared.

Bolan watched the rest of the lambs through, then went to the library.

Leo was sitting on Angeletti's desk, legs swinging, lips thoughtfully pursed.

Bolan strode on past him and to the bar, moved around behind it, opened two cokes.

Leo came up and stood there, gazing at him across the bar.

Bolan shoved a coke over and took off the glasses.

Turrin hissed, *"Motherfucker!"*

Bolan smiled and said, "Glad I was out there."

Leo was beside himself. "God I *thought*—I *looked,* and I—I thought, aw, hell no, couldn't be— you are the *nerviest* bastard I ever . . . the yard boss says you're carrying an *Ace* of *Spades!"*

"That's right," Bolan replied, smiling faintly. "What are you doing here, Leo?"

"Ah, hell, I was ordered to fly down here as some sort of consultant to Angeletti. Just got in a little while ago, took a cab from the airport. These crews were waiting out there . . . I just rode in from the gate with them."

Bolan repeated, "I'm glad I was out there."

"Why, what's the lie?"

"The lie," Bolan explained, "is that those boys are going downstairs for a briefing. And there it is, they just got it." A muffled commotion from below was rattling the floor at their feet.

Leo Turrin turned pale and said, "Choppers."

"Right. And down they went, all in a row."

Turrin grabbed the coke and belted about half of it. Then he wiped his lips with the back of his hand and muttered, "What a lousy way to make a living."

"Yeah," Bolan agreed. "But you're not doing it for that. The world couldn't pay enough for—"

"No way," Turrin growled. "Okay. What's going on? Is this another Palm Springs massacre you're engineering here?"

Bolan said, "Something like that." He went to the window, opened it, looked out.

Sammy the yard boss was trudging back across the lawn, headed for the gate and some fresh blood.

Bolan stepped back to the bar and told his buddy from Pittsfield, "I'll have to watch them in. Can't take a chance on another. . ." The eyes flashed at Turrin. "Wils Brown is supposed to be coming, also."

"Who is Wils Brown?"

"Another guy who knows my face. Friend from back when, black guy. He was counting nickles and dimes for Arnie Farmer last time I—"

"Oh yeah, the NFL guy."

"Not any more," Bolan said. "Not since he threw a block into a Claymore mine . . . in 'Nam."

"He's NFL again," Turrin advised Bolan. "Augie gave me a message for Angeletti. The football guy says go to hell. He left the mob right after that bust of yours in Europe. He's scouting the colleges for the pro's now."

Bolan sighed. "Damn glad to hear that," he muttered.

Another car was moving up the drive.

"Stay put right here," he advised Leo, and went out for the next nose count.

The numbers, the new ones, were coming in now, fast and furious.

The Executioner meant to see that each of them was played to a cadence count.

It was *war*, he kept reminding himself . . . in the *right here and now*.

## Chapter 20/ *The Message*

Regardless of the way the thing eventually worked out, Leo Turrin needed to be covered.

When the last group had been led to the slaughterhouse, Bolan took Sammy and Leo upstairs for a report to the man.

He was seated in a chair at the window, calmly puffing on a cigar.

It was Sammy who told the *Capo*, "It's done, Don Stefano."

"Good work, I'll remember this," Angeletti said lazily. "Give your boys some wine. No—give them whiskey but not too much. And tell them there'll be an extra thousand on their books this month."

The calm gaze swiveled slowly to dwell fully upon Leo Turrin. The eyes flared with a passing uneasiness as he asked, "Who is this?"

Bolan said, "We're in luck, Steven. This is Leopold Turrin from our friends in Massachusetts. They're neutrals. I think Leo should take the message back to New York."

Angeletti proffered his hand. Leo kissed it. The old man became expansive then, smiling and waving the visitor to a chair.

Bolan remained standing. He flicked his eyes at the yard boss and Sammy went out.

The old man said, "I had other ideas for you, Leo, and I thank you for coming but . . . well . . .

no need for that now. What message would you like to take to New York for me?"

Turrin looked at the floor.

He stretched his neck, patted his throat, popped his jaw, bugged his eyes, then patted his throat again.

The old man smiled. "Good, good," he said warmly.

And that was all there was to it.

The Don turned his back on them and resumed his meditative smoking of the cigar.

As Bolan and Turrin returned to the library, Bolan grinned and told his friend, "You're better at that than I am."

"Hell, I was raised in it," Leo said. "I've seen the old guys carry on conversations for hours like that. It's a language all its own."

Bolan knew it.

He also knew what Leo Turrin had told Don Stefano in that weird sign language of the Mafia. He would, he'd indicated, tell the men in New York that Stefano Angeletti was no old man to be dicking around with. He had killed *amici,* yes, but in self-defense and with honor, and he would handle further incursions into his sacred territory in the same manner, with all due respect to the brotherhood.

In the minutes that followed, though, Bolan gave a message of a somewhat different tune for Leo Turrin to carry to New York.

"The old man is addled, stumbling about in his second childhood. He hasn't the faintest notion of what is going on around him, and Frank the Kid is

152

already running things. The Kid has worked out a deal with Don Cafu of Sicily for unlimited support of trained soldiers. He's planning on pulling out of the coalition and setting up a rival shop, and he's gone plain power-crazy. If somebody doesn't look out, Frank the Kid is going to have a standing army of mercenaries from Sicily, and he's going to take over the whole outfit. Or at least, he's going to try."

That was the heart of it. As proof of that pudding, Leo would tell of the treacherous slaughter, by Frank's boys, of the three New York crews who had been dispatched to the aid of Don Stefano. And for no other reason than that they had innocently blundered into Frank's armed takeover of the Angeletti family.

A story such as that may be considered lacking in credibility by ordinary men, but Bolan knew that the New York coalition would buy it—quickly and anxiously. It was merely a repetition of an old, old story played many times upon the Mafia's stages—and playing right now, in varying degrees, throughout the New York City area. The chief variation, in this case, was the use of foreign triggermen—and their presence in the country was already an established fact.

Bolan hoped that the reaction in New York would produce a two-fold result: one, to insure the utter destruction of the Angeletti *Mafiosi* and all their foreign outriders; secondly, to induce the old men in New York to take a new, hard look at this idea of importing foreign guns and at the power which the practice could place in the hands of upstarts like Frank the Kid.

But there was more to Bolan's battle plan than mere *hopes*. Contributing factors in Philadelphia, reacting to Bolan's manipulation of the natural environment there, would add the kicker to make the whole thing jell.

He provided Leo Turrin with an automobile, personally escorted him to the gate, and warmly shook hands with that soldier of the same side.

"Good luck," he said in parting.

"Jesus Christ, keep it for yourself," Turrin replied, and went off to open the second front of Bolan's Philadelphia war.

Frank the Kid was a soaken, sullen heap in the center of his floor, sending murderous glances at the house captain who was working him over with a soggy bath towel.

He wore a terrycloth robe, also soaked, and a steaming cup of coffee was balanced on his thigh.

Bolan told the captain, "Okay, guy, you've earned a rest. Get below, Sammy's setting up drinks."

The guy gave him a grateful and weary smile and got the hell out of there before Bolan could change his mind.

Bolan began rounding up clothing and throwing it at the guy on the floor. "Off your ass," he growled. "We have work to do."

Frank's eyes had dropped to the floor the moment Bolan stepped into the room. Without looking up, he told him, "You've got a hell of a nerve."

"You could use some," Bolan told him. "Your old man facing the toughest night of his life and you dead drunk on your ass through most of it."

Frank's head snapped up and rolled with that verbal punch. The eyes flashed something from the depths which Bolan had never seen there before. He lurched to his feet and went into the bathroom, emerging a moment later with a dry towel. He dried himself and glared at Bolan throughout dressing. Then he told him, "I won't have to put up with this kind of shit forever. Some day you'll be kneeling and kissing my hand."

Bolan said, "In a pig's ass I will. Come on!"

The Kid reluctantly followed the big bastard from the room. As they headed down the hall, he asked, "Where we going?"

"We are going," Bolan replied, "to put a different head on your shoulders."

Frank muttered something beneath his breath and tagged along in silence.

Sammy the yard boss and the house captain were standing just inside the library door, drinks in their hands, talking in low tones.

Each of them started visibly and came to a stiffish attention but Bolan waved his hand at them and said, "Relax, you've earned it," as he and the Kid swept on by.

They went through the kitchen and down the stairs to the basement. A bunch of boys in the ready room were passing a couple of bottles around and laughing it up. They also seemed a bit uncomfortable with the appearance of the bigshots, but one of the guys called out, "Hey, Mr. Cavaretta, have a drink with us."

Bolan grabbed a bottle from an out-thrust hand and faked a belt from it, then passed it to Frank who stiffly handed it on without even a token show of conviviality.

Bolan growled, and pulled him on into the pistol range.

"What're we doing in here?" Frank the Kid complained.

Bolan turned on the lights to the overpowering

smell of spilt blood. Bodies were tumbled everywhere, piled grotesquely, strewn all along that range where earlier victims had been dragged to make room for fresh arrivals. Bolan had counted twenty-six men down those stairs; twenty-six stiffs all in a pile made a hell of an impressive sight.

He did not know what sort of reaction he had been expecting from Frank Angeletti, but he certainly was not expecting the one he got.

The Kid stepped delicately among the victims, carefully avoiding dirtying his shoes with their blood, but grinning and reaching out now and then to turn a face into view. Evidently he was looking for familiar faces and hugely enjoying each one he found.

He did not bother to even ask *why* until he'd picked his way through the entire batch. "What the hell happened here?" he asked, all smiles and good humor now.

Bolan was not entirely surprised, at that. Frank the Kid could be a dangerous son of a bitch if he ever got some legs under him.

And Bolan decided then and there that he could never allow that; his battle plan for the night would have to be revised accordingly.

One beat off the numbers.

He told the Kid, "There's a war on. These boys came down from New York to take you over. We changed their minds."

The damned guy was still grinning. He said, "Yeah, I've sort of been expecting something like that."

157

Bolan gave him a close look, said, "Do tell," and went the hell out of that slaughter pen.

The Judas goat was waiting for them at the door. He glanced at the Kid but directed his worry to the wild card. "What do we do with them guys, Mr. Cavaretta?" he asked.

Bolan replied, "What did Sammy say?"

"Sammy said leave 'em right there 'til you said different."

"It still goes," Bolan said, and went on up the stairs.

Frank had latched onto a bottle on the way out. Bolan had to hurry back and snatch him away from it. He hustled the guy up the stairs and told him, "Touch another bottle tonight and I'll break your face. We have things to do and, dammit, I want you on your legs."

Even that couldn't spoil it for the guy. He chuckled and told Bolan, "Hey, I'm no souse. I just got a little carried away there this evening."

Bolan took him outside and asked him, "Have you been in touch with your Sicily boys since that hit at the Emperor's?"

"Sure. What d'you take me for? It's the first thing I did."

"What's your present head count?"

"What? Oh. Why?"

"Don't be cute, dammit. How many?"

"Well . . . I got twelve stashed in a rooming house over by Connie Mack Stadium. Another fifteen at this other joint. Then there's . . . I got forty-two."

"Out of how many to start with?" Bolan wanted to know.

"None of your damned business."

"Go to hell!" Bolan snarled, turning angrily away. "I didn't come down here to play—"

"Hey, hey!" the Kid yelled. "Okay. I started with seventy-five. So I got hurt, bad. You know what those *malacarni* are costing me? Listen, for every one that dies in my service, I have to send back ten grand *over* the original fee. You think I'm happy about that? For Christ's sake, that hit out there today cost me three hundred gees."

Bolan whistled. This kind of warfare, then, *could* hit them where it hurts. He commented to the Kid. "Hell, if I was your partner, maybe I'd have tied one on myself."

The Kid thought that hilarious. He started to laugh, then cut it off quickly and grabbed the back of his head. "Oh, oh," he said. "Maybe you would but I wouldn't if I had it to do over again. Hey, Johnny. We got off on a bad foot. Let's be friends."

Yeah. A damned dangerous son of a bitch.

Bolan gave him a surprised look and said, "Hell, I never said otherwise, did I?"

"I guess you didn't at that. What're we doing out here in the dark?"

Bolan said, "Talking. Private." And rippling across every key in the repertoire, trying to find a chord for a son of a bitch. "Listen, Frank. You saw that mess in the basement. That's just the beginning, not the end."

"You're on our side I guess, huh?"

Bolan shrugged. "Hell, I have to be neutral, you

know that. But I was sent to advise your papa. That means I advise you, too. You know that. And I think it's time you brought your Sicily boys out of hiding."

Frank was frowning. "I brought 'em out once, and look what happened. The old man took advantage of me. He said the Emperor's would be more defensible. And he wanted to test my boys. He set that up, I know he did. He laid a trail a mile wide from here to there."

"That's past history," Bolan told him. "The thing is, what *he* loses, *you* lose. Right?"

"I guess that's right."

"He's about to lose a lot."

"What do you mean?"

"I mean, dammit—"

"I get you. They picked a good time to lay down on us, didn't they? With this Bolan laying all over us, too. Now *that* guy. . ."

There it was. He saw the look on the Kid's face and told him, "Forget that guy."

"*You* forget 'im. I *saw* the bastard and I'll *never* forget him."

Something turned him, moved him, compelled him, and Bolan voted to risk the exhibit once again. He said, "Come over here and see 'im again then."

He was pulling the guy toward the Maserati.

"What? What are you—?"

"Just shut up and look."

Bolan sprung the lid and opened his prize exhibit for its third premiere showing.

Frank exclaimed, "Well, Jesus! You got the bastard! When did you do that?"

He was all over that prize stiff—feeling, poking, jerking on the combat rig, fooling with the weapons. Bolan took the Beretta and AutoMag away from him and took them to the glove compartment and locked them away.

The guy was still playing with that stiff.

Bolan pushed him aside and closed the exhibit. "When did you get him?"

Bolan growled, "What's important now is he's had. You can forget about that. Right now we have to concentrate on beefing up Carmine and Jules. Those guys are in no strength to take on the New York boys. They need your Sicilians, Frank."

"I'll rent them out," the son of a bitch said.

"I'm ashamed of you, Frank," Bolan said disgustedly.

The guy was still staring at the lid of that luggage compartment. "Be ashamed, then. They're *my* boys and I paid through the nose for them. Would you believe a thousand a *day?* A Goddamned *day?*"

"It's your papa's money, Frank," Bolan pointed out. There was an odd light in Frank the Kid's eyes and Bolan had to wonder who was manipulating whom. "Jules and Carmine are papa's *boys*. Now, what's he going to think if. . ."

"Okay, okay," Frank said, laughing and trying to pass the thing off as a joke. "You know I wouldn't hold out at a time like this. Johnny. . . . What're you going to do with that guy?"

Right. Dangerous, very!

"What guy?"

Frank threw a glance at the Maserati. "That guy."

"I'll be taking him in."

"In where?"

"Hell, back to the head-shed. There's a hundred thou' on that boy."

"Sell him to me."

"What?"

"Let me take him in. For the *family*—our pride. It would help us in this time we're having. Don't you think? How many families has this boy made monkeys of? Just about all of them. Right? It would help us here in Philly if . . . Johnny, I'll do anything you say. But let *me* take him in. Naturally I'll turn the contract purse over to you."

"Oh, hell, I don't know," Bolan said.

"I'll give you the purse and add ten of my own. Make it twenty. Whatever you think is right."

Bolan repeated, "I don't know. It's more than money. It's like you said, *pride* too. I mean, you know. The boy that got *this* boy is going to be something special. You know?"

Damn right Frank knew.

The idea was full into his gut now and it was tearing him apart. He was shaking all over as he told the wild card from New York, "Name your price, just name it. Johnny, I've *got* to have this boy."

Bolan hesitated as long as the moment would allow, then he told Frank the Kid Getting Legs Under Him, "Well, I guess money isn't everything, is it? Like you say, people will be kissing your hands

162

some day. You won't forget me when that day comes, will you, Frank?"

"Listen, you know better. Anything you ever want, Johnny . . ."

"Okay, just give me the purse. But you better give it to me now. Just to keep things straight."

"You want it now? All of it now?"

Bolan stretched his neck and popped a burp into his palm. "Well, if you can put your hands on that much, yeah."

"Oh, hell, I *can*. Johnny . . . does Don Stefano know? About . . .?"

Bolan assured him, "Oh you're the first to know."

"Okay." The guy was soaring. "It's between you and me, then, and it's going to stay that way. From now on it's Frankie and Johnny, right? Hey, those two names go together. Look, I got the money. I was planning another trip to Sicily and I got the cash stashed. Johnny, I'm going to give you a hundred and ten."

"That's damn big of you, Frank. But the hundred's okay."

"No, you're going to get the extra. Listen, wait right here, we'll seal this deal right now."

Bolan halted the guy as he was starting to trot toward the house. He said, "Keep it quiet, Frank. One guys knows and it blows the whole thing."

"Shit, don't worry."

"While you're in there . . . this is important . . . call your crew bosses. Send half to Jules, half to Carmine. Be sure and do that, Frank, because they may not have much time left."

"I will, honest to Christ, I will."

The guy hit the back door on the run.

Bolan leaned against the Maserati and rubbed his eyes.

It was an Executioner's never-never land, and a melody played by ear had never sounded sweeter.

## Chapter 22/ *Numbers Falling*

They transferred Bolan's side of the $110,000 transaction to the trunk of Frank Angeletti's Buick —with necessary modifications—and Bolan rode with the guy as far as the gate.

Frank was bubbling over from head to toe, already living the fantasy of "the man who got Mack Bolan"—he could hardly wait to begin the victorious trek to *Commissione* headquarters in New York.

For the third time Bolan had inquired and was reassured regarding the disposition of Frank's Sicilians. They were on their way, the Kid swore, half of them going to join Jules Sticatta, the other half to Carmine Drasco.

Bolan stepped out at the gate and sent the conquering hero off with a wink, and he was hurrying back to the house when a scuffle on the front lawn commanded his attention.

Some guy over there was getting the hell beat out of him, or so it looked. Three of the yardmen had the guy on the ground and were giving it to him with fists and feet when Bolan broke into the fray and began pulling boys off.

"Lousy cop!" one of the guys yelled.

So it was. The young plain-clothes man whose path Bolan had repeatedly crossed that day now lay at his feet.

The guy's eyes blazed up at Bolan and he was

breathing like a steam engine, mad as hell—probably more so at himself than anything else.

Bolan pulled the guy to his feet, brushed him off, examined him for damages and found none. He'd probably have tender ribs and a sore belly for a day or so, but he'd live through it.

The dignity, though—that might be another matter.

A hardman was dangling the cop's revolver from a finger, giving Bolan a questioning stare.

Bolan accepted the gun and jammed it into the guy's holster. He told him, "You can't blame the boys for jumping you. It's your neck that's out, you know. You have no business in here. That was no annual permit you boys brought in here tonight."

Sammy had heard the commotion also and was coming running. He slowed at the sight of Bolan/Cavaretta, sized up the situation and said, "Geez, now what?"

Bolan replied, "Now, nothing. The guy was just leaving."

The yard boss protested, "Hell, Johnny, if the guy has been prowling around here . . . well, I don't know."

"Nah, it's okay," Bolan said. "The guy wants the same thing we want. He's a soldier of the same side. Right? Beat it, cop. Good hunting."

The detective spun about, without a word, and headed for the wall.

Sammy's face was twisted with an inner torment. He cried, "Mr. Cavaretta, I don't think—"

Bolan snapped, "No you don't! That's my department! He goes!"

The cop went, and Bolan continued on to the house.

It was an incident he could have done without.

He needed to get damn quick to the telephone and get some more numbers into the game.

He went directly to the library and picked up the desk phone just as someone somewhere else in the house was hanging up an extension.

Bolan re-cradled the instrument, his gaze shifting to the ceiling directly overhead, then he picked it up again.

He got a no-interference dial-tone but again waited several seconds, then called the number which Drasco had left with him.

Carmine himself answered the first ring. Bolan told him, "This is me. You know what is coming at you right now, this very minute. You better be ready."

Drasco's cautious reply was reassuring. "Thanks, we are. How many?"

"Forty-two all told. Half to you, half to Jules. You better call him."

"Okay. You know we appreciate it."

Bolan said, "Wait. I heard this much, also. What's that recognition signal you boys been using?"

"You mean with the lights?"

"Yeah."

"Okay, well, just two clicks high beam and hold, two clicks low and hold, another high and fast back to low."

"That's the one," Bolan said, hoping so. "Watch for that. It means something else tonight. It's their signal to each other. It means everything looks okay, crash right in."

"They'll crash, all right," Drasco muttered, and hung up.

Smiling solemnly, Bolan consulted the telephone directory and made another call, reached his party after some haggling over names and departments, quickly had his say, and hung up.

Then he went upstairs to see why the Don was playing with the telephone.

Captain Thomkins was hunched over his desk, staring glumly into a pint carton of milk. He told Joe Persicone, "When they bury me, I want them to make my tombstone out of recycled milk cartons and sandwich wraps. I've spent half my life in their company, I may as well go on through eternity that way."

The FBI man was stretched across two chairs. He shifted his feet and grunted a tired groan. "We may as well hang it up, Wayne. I think we missed our guess. I don't think we'll ever hear of the guy again."

"Don't start that," Thompkins growled. "I haven't given up yet."

As if to reward his perseverence, Bolan's call came at that precise instant.

The Captain snatched up the phone and his eyes found the interested gaze of Persicone as he said, "Yeah, yeah, this is the big cop in the dirty gray suit. Who's this?"

The eyes blinked at the FBI man as he said, *"Who?"*

168

Persicone kicked his feet clear and slid to the edge of his chair.

The cop was saying, "Sure, I know where. You say there'll be—wait! How do I know you're really who you say you are?" The eyes crackled. "Okay, fella. Hey! Do me a personal favor, will you? Get the hell out of our town!"

The FBI agent could hear the crisp crackling of the telephone receiver, the methodical voice that rattled it.

The Captain's eyes were alternately narrowing and widening, in some weird rhythm of attentive listening.

Finally Thomkins yelled, "Wait, dammit! Did he —? He *did*!" He flung the telephone down and said, "He hung up on me!"

"Who did he say was calling?" Persicone inquired, knowing already.

"He said it was Mack Bolan. He said the foreign army, what the hell ever that is, is storming the hall of horrors, whatever the hell *that* is, and we should rush right out to Drasco's and Sticatta's— ready to pick up the pieces."

Persicone was on his feet. He said, "Well? Are we going?"

"Well, wait, I want to. . ."

"I think we should."

"I already have a force at each place. Let me. . ."

"Was that all he said?"

"It's not all he said. I hope I got a recording of that. He says we should send fingerprints on all those mala—macaroni or something to—"

169

*"Malacarni?"*

"That's the one. What's it mean?"

"I'll tell you later. Go on, what else did he say?"

"We should send these fingerprints to Interpol, we might be very interested in the results. Joe. . . ?"

The Captain was giving the FBI man a very searching gaze.

Persicone found it discomforting. He said, "What?"—a bit testily.

"Level with me. Is this guy working with you people?"

"Bolan? You know better! Come on, what else?"

Thomkins sighed. "He just said the numbers were falling. And he hung up."

Persicone was fidgeting, at the door. "I think we should go."

"You're convinced it was him?" the Captain asked.

"It was," Persicone sighed, "for *damned sure* him."

The Don was seated at the window, precisely as Bolan had left him earlier, except that a telephone rested upon his lap. He was staring at it and humming, sort of, a discordant tune.

Bolan had him in the side view, the tired old features in sharp profile. They were tired with good reason. Stefano Angeletti had been one of the busiest and nastiest hoods in the business for nearly fifty years. He'd hacked his way through that jungle of deceit and brutality, giving more suffering than getting, and he'd made it through that jungle at the head of the pack in a crowded and viciously competitive field.

But it had been a rotten trip—and the evidence of that was all hanging out, here, tonight, in this time and place. The ravages of fifty years behind the footlights were there for anyone to see, and Bolan was seeing a lot.

The pity of it all was that the guy was still in that jungle—he hadn't made it through anything except fifty years of sheer survival.

And the guy was sitting there humming a song—a song of something. Something, no doubt, as rotten as himself.

Bolan leaned against the wall, arms crossed, and asked the humming man, "Trying to conjure up a call, Stefano?"

"I already had my call," the old man quietly replied.

Bolan bent down to take the phone. He did so, and an ugly little black revolver replaced it in Angeletti's hand.

In that same motion, a silencer-tipped Browning auto slipped its snout between Angeletti's lips.

It was not exactly a Mexican stand-off. Bolan could have blasted him then and there, or so he figured, and walked away. . . maybe. But there was something in those watery old eyes that stayed him, and pulled him back, and instead he told the *Capo*, "I'll wait if you will."

"You got longer than me," the Don replied in a very dry voice.

Bolan said, "That must have been some call."

"It was and it wasn't."

Bolan carefully put the phone on the table and leaned a shoulder against the wall, the Browning there and ready.

"I got one and I sent one," Angeletti was telling him, in a voice so tired it almost wasn't there. "Philippa called to say good-bye. She's not coming back, she says. But blood is thicker than water, isn't it? *Our* kind of blood, I don't know about yours. She told me I should check you out. Said you had buckshot wounds, and it was bothering her." He cackled but those eyes never left Bolan's trigger finger. "Imagine that. She was worried about her Papa."

Bolan said, "Well, it figures, doesn't it?"

The old man went on as though he had not heard the comment. "So I called Augie. I would've

172

called earlier, I was going to. But the damn phones were out. Then by the time they came back in—hell, guy, by then you had me up your tree but good, didn't you? So I called Augie. He says this Johnny Cavaretta didn't leave there until late. Couldn't possibly get here before six. Not possible, he says. I'm gonna put a bullet right up your nose, mister smart-ass. Whatta you think about that?"

Bolan shrugged his free shoulder. "It comes to all of us, Steven. Question now is—which of us first? Even without me, though, yours is on the way. What did Augie have to say about your temporary insanity?"

"You crazy? I told Augie nothing! I got to figure out the damage you did, first."

Bolan wondered if the old man was still in touch with reality. He seemed to have lost the awareness of the Browning.

"Irreversible," he told the Don.

"What?"

"The damage is irreversible. Can't be patched up. One way you look at it, Stefano, you're a total ass. The other way, you hauled off and wiped out the delegations from three friendly families for no good reason at all. Unless maybe you're trying for a takeover."

"Aaagh, you think—"

"Or unless Frank is."

"What? What'd you say?"

Bolan shrugged the free shoulder. "It could look like Frank the Kid is trying for a takeover."

"Nobody will ever know," the old guy said, his

voice sinking again. "You'll get all the credit for those dead boys down there."

"No good, Steven. It'll never hang together. Anybody seeing that mess down there will know what happened. They'll know I couldn't have engineered something like that. Besides, it has your brand all over it. And too many boys know what really happened here tonight."

The gray chin was quivering, eyes watering. "What other kind of dirt have you been doing here under my nose?"

"Not much more. Except that Jules and Carmine are right now fighting for their lives against Frank's Sicilians."

The old man lunged forward in the chair and cried, "What!?"

Bolan nodded and watched that gun hand. "That's right."

The hammer of the revolver was back and ready, the snout angling at Bolan's face. He saw the hand that held it shake, and he was tensing into his own pull.

But it didn't come off. The old man wasn't through with him yet. "That stiff you showed me," he was asking. "Is that Johnny Cavaretta?"

Bolan nodded. "It is."

The hand shook some more.

Bolan could appreciate the emotional pressures building inside that tired old head. This was a bitter pill for a bigshot boss like Angeletti to have to swallow—the overnight destruction of everything he'd labored to pull together for the past fifty years. Yeah, there were plenty of emotions there.

He thought, *what the hell?*—and tossed in another number for contemplation.

"I sold it to Frank," he said.

"You did what?"

"I sold the stiff to Frank the Kid."

"What the hell would he want with—?"

"Well, just the head. Easier to handle. He dumped the rest in the basement."

"Oh . . . *God!*"

"Besides, walking in with just a head is classier. You can toss it on a guy's desk and snap your fingers and say hey, look what I brought in."

"Oh, God, *no!*"

The old boy hadn't lost touch with anything. He'd picked that up damn quick . . . and he knew . . . he knew. All the pain and heartbreak and anxiety over a kid and heir with no legs at all under him broke through that massive hatred and anger, that bitter will to survive and punish. He was shuddering all over as he asked the Executioner, "Has he already left?"

"He's left," Bolan said quietly.

"Go get him *back!*" Angeletti screamed. "You can do it! I'll give you anything—I'll give you everything I got! Just don't let the kid do that to hisself. No telling what they'll think! Or do! My God, that guy was a *Talifero! Dammit, you run get 'im back!*"

Bolan leaned down and plucked the revolver from limp fingers and thrust it into his waistband.

"No way, Steven," he said. "That one was my grand-slammer."

There was no way for Stefano Angeletti, either.

175

The yelling fit or the new hopelessness or something had defeated him and he sank back into the cushions of the chair with a rattling sigh, hardly a drop of gas left in his tank.

"You'll get yours some day, guy," the old man promised the Executioner. The eyes were looking yellow now, blazing purest hatred as though all the strength of an abused lifetime had been consolidated into that moment.

Bolan sighed and said, "Don't we all," and turned to leave.

The house captain came through the doorway about then, attracted probably by the old man's emotional shouting.

Stefano spent his last drop of gas to whimper, "Take him, Tony! God, *take* him!"

"Take *who?*" the houseman asked, the face that had suffered the idiosyncrasies of this inner family group for perhaps half a lifetime twisting in patient puzzlement.

Bolan showed the guy a sad smile and told him, "He thinks I'm Mack Bolan."

"Oh, Jesus," the guy whispered, and backed out of there shaking his head.

Bolan paused in the doorway for a parting look at success, Mafia-style.

Don Stefano Angeletti was bent forward on his throne, leathery hands clutching at the mahogany arms.

"Kill me, you prick!" he wheezed.

"I already killed you, Steven," Bolan told the Don, then he went away from there, down to the carport, into the Maserati.

A familiar figure detached itself from the shadows as he was cranking the engine, and Sammy the yard boss stepped to the side of the vehicle.

"You checking out, Mr. Cavaretta?" the yardman asked, the voice a trifle uneasy.

Bolan grinned as he replied, "Right, and you haven't even learned to call me Johnny."

"I guess I never would," Sammy told him. "Uh . . . the house captain told me about the Don. Is he . . . is he . . .?"

"He's alive," Bolan assured the guy. "Listen, Sammy . . ."

The yard boss was giving him an anguished, sorrowful gaze—and Bolan was gazing back but he was seeing instead of Sammy a little tag-man at Las Vegas—Max Keno by name, instant-loyalty by game—and he knew that Max and Sammy were formed from the same mold. Nothing particularly admirable . . . not especially bad . . . they were just . . .

Guys like this had never been torpedoes or hitmen or squeeze-men; they'd spent their lifetimes in loyal service to a cause they didn't even understand —and they served a crown, not the man beneath it. Soldiers of the court, spending most of their days and nights just standing around to make some rotten old man feel important and deserving of kisses upon the hand.

Soldiers of the *other* side. But soldiers, still.

Bolan sighed and quit wrestling with himself. For Max, then—and probably for Sammy as well, he told the guy, "The old man is alive and he isn't, Sammy. You'd better go up and sit with him. The stage is falling in."

177

"What is?"

"All of it, the whole lousy hall of horrors is tumbling down. Put the old man to bed . . . then you better round up all your boys and either split or get as hard as you know how, because tomorrow is going to be some kind of hell day around here, believe me."

"I—God, I knew something was sour. A crew of your boys just relieved us down at the gate. I guess I knew. . . ."

Bolan felt a familiar iciness enveloping his heart. He kept the voice casual, though, as he inquired, "What crew is that, Sammy?"

"*Taliferi*. Crew boss is a guy named Chianto. Uh, does this mean that we're . . . ? Uh, Frank is . . . ?"

"Frank won't be coming back," Bolan muttered. "Neither will Philippa if she has the brains I think she has. Naw. It's falling, Sammy. Get your boys together, cross your fingers, and sit tight."

The guy was obviously confused but he said, "Thanks. I—thanks, Johnny."

The Maserati was already in motion, gliding silently along the drive toward the gate.

So. One of those chance numbers had dropped into the game, and now it was all numbers up for grabs.

This could be a reaction to the "second front" effort he'd sent to New York with Leo Turrin. If so, then this elite crew of *Commissione* enforcers had already been on hand, in the background somewhere, hovering, awaiting a signal to join the game in Philadelphia. Maybe they had even come down with the real Johnny Cavaretta. Whatever and however, it was one of those unpredictables which Bolan had been gambling against . . . and twice in the same night he had pushed his chances one number too many.

There would be no brazening past these boys . . . not the *Taliferi*. Whatever they had come for, they would most likely tumble quickly to the fact that something was very much out of place, and they would certainly not be politely "sirring" Bolan through that gate down there.

One thing would inevitably lead to another . . . and maybe another head would go rolling toward Manhattan on this night of nights.

A crew wagon, one of the big eight-passenger limousines, had been pulled well inside the grounds and was parked on the grass beside the drive.

A door was open and a guy was sitting in that open doorway, his feet on the ground. He would, Bolan knew, be cuddling either a shotgun or a chopper between his legs.

Two guys were flanking the vehicle, standing casually at either end, hands on hips.

Four more were down at the gate, two to each side, arms folded across chests—hands very close to concealed pistol grips.

So. Seven in plain sight. Another one or two, probably, skulking somewhere in the shadows.

And the time had come for "combat quick"— frontal assault with all the stops pulled—no cuteness, no finesse, but simple and brutal battlefield-style bust-out.

He had already sprung the AutoMag from its confinement in the glove compartment. Now he added the Beretta, unmuzzled. The Maserati's door eased open and Bolan rolled out, the vehicle continuing to creep along the drive, unpiloted.

The maneuver gave him a one-number edge. For a split second the forty-G shark ran interference and provided a screen between Bolan and the enemy.

There were warning cries and sprinting men moving in all directions when that screen passed on —then the Executioner was on both feet and moving them in a demonstration of open-field running which would probably have swelled the football heart of his old buddy Wilson Brown.

The guy who had stayed with the crew wagon was the first target up. He was whirling alongside the limousine, trying to get a Thompson into play across the engine hood.

The AutoMag roared flame and thunder, and blew point-blank massive death into the guy's face. The Thompson chattered briefly at the moon as it disappeared behind the vehicle with its dead programmer.

The other two guys at the car had flung themselves onto the grass. One was still rolling for darkness; the other had come to one knee and was unloading a revolver in quick-fire at a target which just would not hold still. The second sizzling magnum from the silver .44 blasted straight into the guy's wide-open mouth and punched him over onto his back.

An instantaneous crack from the Beretta found

the rolling man and ended his journey in a grotesque pile-up of arms and legs.

The four who had been at the gate were commanding attention with a crackling of fire from the wall at either side of the gate. Several missiles plowed simultaneously into the turf in the path of Bolan's advancing feet and another sang past his ear, carrying a sample of Executioner skin—from the cheek—along with it.

A rapid-fire retort from both of Bolan's weapons brought quick disorganization down there, plus a groan from one quarter and a cry of "I'm hit!" from another.

In that same moment, Bolan discerned motion in his side vision and another muzzle-flash from the darkness behind him served as an announcement for the tearing pain that penetrated his left leg and sent him sprawling. The next roar of the .44 sent a screaming sizzler unerringly along the backtrack of fire and found live meat in that darkness, the connection signaled by another agonized cry.

Someone along the wall had yelped, "He's down! He's hit!" and another volley of hand-gun fire tore turf all about him.

Instinctively Bolan was rolling for shadow and blindly returning fire, very much aware that he was bleeding from two places but also strongly aware that he'd cut the odds down to a much more manageable two-to-one.

Some men die easily, passively, passing back through the gateway of life with a gentle sigh or despairing moan.

Some die with great reluctance, angrily, snatch-

181

ing at everything within reach to block that narrow passageway and to seal themselves into the *Life* side.

Bolan was one of those latter.

He reached the shadow of the wall and surged to his feet, shaking off a wave of pain and nausea from the protesting leg, and went on without pause toward his goal.

He saw the whites of the enemy's eyes and heard the guy's shuddering gasps for life mingling with the metallic clicks of a firing pin upon spent cartridges.

The hammer of the AutoMag itself fell upon an empty chamber; instinctively the left trigger finger closed that fist and the Beretta sent her last charge into shattering flesh and bone—and Bolan was moving past the guy as he fell.

Then it was just Bolan, the iron gate, and the Maserati which had sputtered to a halt just uprange, and maybe one more gunner directly across the drive—a very silent gunner, at the moment.

He punched the button to activate the gate at the same instant that he plunged inside the jacket for Cavaretta's Browning. But the Browning, not too securely leathered for this type of play, had dropped off somewhere back there—and, yeah, there was one more gunner over there.

In one of those flashing moments of the combat sense the guy had become aware that Bolan's weapons were empty. He stepped into the gateway, smiling triumphantly, a long-barreled revolver held in both hands and extended at arm's length, tracking coolly on the big man's defensive whirl.

Bolan was not spinning into an escape path, however. He was closing for hand-to-hand combat and the guy misread it, sending his first round into the empty space which Bolan had just vacated.

Then the big silver auto was whizzing through the gap, airborne and directly on target, and the gunner's second shot was spoiled as he flinched away from the impact.

Bolan himself had closed that gap.

The guy's revolver went spinning into darkness an instant before he found himself locked into a spine-cracking bearhug.

The gunner gurgled, "God, wait!"

But God or the universe had obviously waited long enough, and another *Taliferi* died instantly in Mack Bolan's embrace.

Bolan let the guy fall away and he took a couple of faltering steps toward the Maserati before recognizing the urgency of the frantic signals surging up from his injured limb.

The battle had been furious, but swift. Mere seconds had elapsed since he'd piled out of that rolling vehicle. Not quite long enough to bleed to death—but quite long enough for shock and weakness to begin settling in through that determined search for Life.

He dropped to one knee to examine the wound, probing with both hands. It was a flesh hit, luckily —no bone involvement, a tearing wound along the calf—but bleeding like hell. Somehow the scarf he'd taken from Johnny Cavaretta had remained

183

with him. He removed it from his shoulders and used it to tourniquet the bleeding leg.

Blood was also oozing from the gouge along his right cheek, but this hit was more painful than dangerous. He tore off a corner of the scarf and used it to dab at the face wound, and only then did he discover that the last shot of the battle had not gone completely astray. It had struck the gun-leather beneath his left arm and angled into the flesh to lodge between skin and ribs; Bolan could feel it in there, could trace the outline of the slug with his finger. And, yeah, he was bleeding some there, also.

He was hobbling toward the Maserati when the other guy appeared, seemingly from nowhere, standing dead-center in the open gateway.

It was, sure—the young detective.

How now, big bad Bolan?

He scowled at the guy, then his chin fell and he showed the cop empty hands and said, "Zero."

The guy knelt to scoop something off the pavement, then came over and shoved it into the waistband of Bolan's trousers. It was the AutoMag.

The cop was smiling soberly. He said, "Zero, hell," and helped the Executioner to the waiting forty-grand shark.

He closed the door on the most wanted man in America and asked him, "Got a light?"

Bolan wordlessly passed over a packet of matches.

The cop lit a cigarette, handed it to Bolan, and told him, "Never can remember to bring enough matches for overtime."

Bolan took a drag and threw a glance toward the

house as he exhaled. He could see men standing at the windows up there.

The cop was lighting another cigarette. He blew the smoke toward the house and asked, "Is it true a bigshot Mafia Don owns this joint?"

Bolan grinned sourly and replied, "How the hell should I know? I've just been looking for a friend."

"Looks like you found him," the cop said. He pressed a scrap of cloth into Bolan's hand. "I was saving this, as a war souvenir. Guess it's not worth much as evidence. You better take it, as a souvenir of Philly. You're leaking out of your left side, maybe you better use it as a patch."

Bolan was inspecting the cloth as the guy spoke. It was a pocket from his black-suit. "Where'd you find this?" he asked.

"It's off a soldier of the same side, I guess. How the hell should I know? It was growing out of a tree over there somewhere. You'd better beat it, soldier. You'll be getting in the law's way here, most any minute now. Good hunting. Uh, if I were driving this bomb, I'd veer right at the gate and not look back until I was crossing Franklin Bridge."

Bolan cranked the engine, thanked the cop with his eyes, and put that place behind him.

So it was ending on a decent note.

He was taking more than a torn pocket away as a souvenir of Philadelphia. He was carrying lead and pain and shredded flesh as well—but that was nothing particularly new. The important thing that he was carrying out of Philadelphia was a good feeling, a hell of a good feeling.

The Executioner's part of it was finished. But the melody of his visit would linger on—and the panic in Philadelphia, he knew, was getting stronger by the hour.

A night for miracles? Bolan shook his head and ran a finger along the outline of the bullet at his ribs. Miracles, he knew, could happen anywhere, everywhere—any time the human spirit *moved* and *tried*.

He knew, also, that tomorrow and a whole string of tomorrows were going to be some kind of hellish days for the Angeletti *Mafiosi*.

Yeah. He was carrying something precious away from the city of brotherly love.

He was carrying life, largely lived.

## EPILOG

He'd crossed the Delaware via the Ben Franklin Bridge and made tracks for the New Jersey Turnpike. The forty-G shark was devouring two full miles per minute and not even straining when the news from Philadelphia broke the airwaves to assure the Executioner that all the numbers had come home in the city of brotherly love.

He listened to the news, smoked a cigarette, and let the Maserati take its own head.

He had no clear idea of where he was going, nor what he would do if he ever arrived there.

It seemed a fairly safe bet, though, that somewhere up there in that immediate and uncertain future lay a trail which would lead him to a guy called Don Cafu and possibly a return bout with the *gradigghia* on their home turf.

Sicily, he'd heard, was beautiful this time of year.

Bolan had everything he'd need for a safari into the enemy's ancestral jungles.

He had the bounty he'd collected on a bounty hunter—a hundred and ten big ones—a good car under him, and the name of a guy in New York who provided passports and special travel arrangements for a special fee.

He also had the name of a medic in the big city who would patch up gunshot damage without qualms or questions.

He did not need much else. Except his nerve, his numbers, and a willing universe.

Yeah. Sicily was supposed to be very pretty this time of year. And the hunting, he'd heard, was excellent.

POLICE BUSINESS
**RESTRICTED COMMUNIQUE**
SCRAMBLE CIRCUIT AUTHY #PH105
FROM PHILA PD/TF 142351L
TO H BROGNOLA/USDOJ/WASHDC
**IMMEDIATE ATTN**BOLAN**
BT
SUBJECT BELIEVED DEPARTED PHILA
THIS DATE, DESTINATION UNKNOWN.
MAFIA DON STEFANO ANGELETTI
ENTIRE ORG APPEARS IN TOTAL
DISARRAY, SCORES DEAD, HOSPITALIZED,
OR UNDER ARREST. REMNANTS
REPORTED DISPERSING IN PANIC IN
EXPECTATION OF RETALIATION FROM
OTHER ORGCRIME ELEMENTS
ADJACENT AREAS, REASONS UNDISCLOS-
ED AT THIS TIME. AGENT PERSICONE
SUGGESTS POSSIBLE QUOTE BOLAN
TWIST UNQUOTE SIMILAR TO PALM
SPRINGS HIT. SUBJECT POSSIBLY
TRAVELING UNDER IDENTIFICATION
JOHN J CAVARETTA WITH COMMISSIONE
CREDENTIALS BUT UNLIKELY TO
CONTINUE THIS GUISE BEYOND
IMMEDIATE PHILA AREA. REQUEST
IMMEDIATE AND OFFICIAL
CLARIFICATION SICILIAN TERMS

GRADIGGHIA AND MALACARNI ALSO
REQUEST FED FOLLOW-UP SPECIAL
FINGERPRINT ID REQUEST TELEFAXED
THIS DATE.
BT
THOMPKINS/PERSICONE PHILA SEND
FROM BOTTLE AND BEDSPRINGS.
                    END OF MESSAGE

# the Executioner

The gutsiest, most exciting hero in years. Imagine a guy at war with the Godfather and all his Mafioso relatives! He's rough, he's deadly, he's a law unto himself — nothing and nobody stops him!

## THE EXECUTIONER SERIES by DON PENDLETON

# Violence is a man! His name is Edge...

The bloodiest action-series ever published, with a hero who is the meanest, most vicious killer the West has ever seen.

### It's sharp —
### It's hard —
### It's EDGE

| Order | | Title | Book No. | Price |
|---|---|---|---|---|
| _____ | #1 | The Loner | P109N | 95¢ |
| _____ | #2 | Ten Grand | P115N | 95¢ |
| _____ | #3 | Apache Death | P133N | 95¢ |
| _____ | #4 | Killer's Breed | P148N | 95¢ |

more to come...